Murder on Rosemary Street

By Mary Fulk Larson

Cover Photography by Tammy Cullers
Cover Design by Kevin Finnegan

Printed in the United States
First Edition
Library of Congress Control Number: 2015919687
ISBN-9-780692-546321

Visit Custer's Mill Mysteries on Facebook
or at www.custersmillmystery.com

Prologue
July 4, 1985

Kath's head was killing her. It had been a long day at the diner and not even a small breeze stirred the humid air. Her skin felt damp and sticky. She walked up the porch steps of the house she shared with her mother and daughter and paused a moment. The peeling blue paint and broken screen door were not as obvious in the dim moonlight, in fact, they gave the dilapidated house a certain charm.

Kath opened the door and stepped inside, avoiding the light switch by the corner of the kitchen, her head pounding loudly in her ears in rhythm to her heartbeat. She was thankful her mother had taken Mirabelle to the fireworks tonight. Light was not Kath's friend when she had a migraine. Hopefully, a good night's sleep would take care of this hellish headache. The oppressive heat made it worse.

She made her way down the hallway, careful to step around two-year-old Mirabelle's doll and some pans she'd been playing with that morning. Inside her small bedroom, Kath stripped off her moist blouse and eased herself onto the bed, sighing with relief when her head reached the pillow. The heavy-duty meds her mother had given her would soon ease the pain. Come on, sleep, she begged.

At last, Kath began to relax and soon she was deeply asleep.

As she slept, three figures slipped through the woods that bordered the lawn, stepping gingerly to avoid snapping twigs or startling night animals. The songs of tree frogs and crickets filled the night air. Explosions of fireworks popped erratically in the distance.

The tallest of the three carried a gasoline can. As they reached the small garden shed next to the house, one figure lagged behind and stood unmoving. The leader of the group made a violent gesture toward him, and spat out whispered instructions. The tall one poured fuel around the perimeter of the small building and stepped back in line with the others.

A sudden brightness illuminated their faces as they hurled lit firecrackers toward a wheelbarrow leaning against the wall of the shed. Successive explosions rang out, and bright flames raced along the trail of gasoline. The small building was soon engulfed in fire. The leader gestured toward the woods with a jerk of his thumb and hissed a low command. The figures ran swiftly to safety.

Pausing at the edge of the woods, they watched in silence as the fire crept along the interior of the little building. The flames glowed eerily through the grimy windows. Satisfied, they disappeared into the trees.

Some distance away, a man leaned against a black walnut tree and stubbed out his cigarette on the rough bark. His dad was drinking again tonight—celebrating, he called it. You know, the Fourth of July. Freedom. It was best to stay out of the house until Dad passed out.

An almost-full moon scattered shadows through the trees.

Suddenly, the man glimpsed three figures emerging from the woods along the steep bank, north of the old Alger farm lane. Nobody used that lane anymore. There was just enough light to see the forms running swiftly along the lower edge of the bank toward a car parked about a hundred feet from where he stood. As they approached, he recognized their faces in the moonlight, and heard a deep voice curse angrily as the car doors opened and then closed. The voice, too, was familiar.

The engine revved, and the car drove away slowly, headlights off, crunching over the gravel. Curious, he thought.

The smell of smoke filled the night air as a loud explosion echoed through the woods.

Chapter 1
May, 2012

Bertha Brubaker had not been this excited in all of her eighty-three years! If she believed in fate, she would have sworn that all the astral bodies had lined up in perfect order to steer Lady Luck in her direction. She glanced into the old Victorian mirror in the foyer and adjusted her straw hat. Her cheeks were pink from anticipation. She looked at the small glass vial on the edge of the buffet. Should she? No, probably not. She felt perky this morning, even without old Bessie Crawford's herbal infusion. She'd save that mix of herbs for another day.

She patted the large leather tote bag at her side and squinted at the ancient grandfather clock in the corner of the sitting room. She was grateful she'd found the letter in the trunk while she still had time. With a bit of luck she could get down to the library basement, juggle the toggles on the vault lock, and pull out the documents before anybody asked questions. Not that Bertha would keep her secret forever. In fact, she was looking forward to revealing it to the world. But all in good time. All in proper order.

At the moment, all she had to do was get past Hiram Steinbacher, her eagle-eyed gardener. She had seen him earlier today, hoeing the redroot from the begonia beds, his long, graying hair pulled back into a ponytail beneath a ratty old baseball cap. His whiskered, weathered face made him look much older than he was. Around forty-five, Bertha guessed. He had gone to school with her nephew, Billy. Hiram had been Bertha's employee for over twenty years, but she didn't want him prying into her business today. He'd asked enough questions when she'd had him bring that old trunk down from the attic. Funny how he could be so silent about his own affairs and so nosy about hers.

"You're out early, Miss."

Bertha sighed. She should have known she couldn't get by without Hiram seeing her. He should have been an undercover detective . . . or a country preacher. She'd certainly suffered through enough of his impromptu sermons.

"Some errands to run, Hiram. I'm getting an early start before the day heats up."

"Already hot." Hiram took off his dirty cap and passed a grimy hand over his forehead. "Though nothing like the lakes of fire that await the wicked!"

"Speaking of hot, your daughter, Sissy, told me that you're still living in that filthy green vehicle. You must be burning up in there at night!" Bertha nodded toward a rusty Chevy van partially hidden by a sprawling rosebush.

Hiram grunted and raised his steely blue eyes to meet Bertha's gaze. "Miss, as long as my girl and her man insist on having that tool of the devil in their house, I'll live in my van. The Good Book says if your eye causes you to sin, pluck it out. That devil-vision they call a TV would make a blind man out of me."

"TV is like any other invention; it can be used for good or evil." Bertha glanced at her watch. She couldn't believe she was wasting time listening to Hiram's rants.

"I'd be hard pressed to find anything good about that wicked picture show. No God-fearing man would sit down and feast his eyes on the filth that runs across the screen."

This conversation was going nowhere. Bertha turned to walk away. "I reckon when it gets cold you'll be grateful enough for your daughter's trailer. And please, Hiram, use the shower in the guest cottage to clean up. There's no call for you to smell like a barnyard."

"More to life than comfort. Eye for an eye . . . tooth for a tooth . . ." His voice trailed off as he turned back toward the rose bush he was trimming.

Bertha shook her head. Well, at least she had made it past him without having to tell him where she was headed. She still had her gift of controlling conversations. A small, satisfied smile tugged at the corners of her mouth.

The path from the Brubaker estate to Custer's Mill Library was smooth, but the incline from the street curb to the top of the steps winded Bertha. By the time she opened the library door, she was completely out of breath. Old Doc Nash might have given her a clean bill of health at her last checkup, but she was feeling every one of her eighty-three years this morning. She pulled a lace handkerchief from her tote bag and wiped her brow.

Volunteers Nanette Steele and Jane Allman were working in the back of the library. Bertha tightened her lips in irritation. These ladies were some of her best friends, but they could be such busybodies—especially Nanette! Bertha was convinced that the woman kept files on every citizen in Custer's Mill. Well, at least they hadn't seen her. Not yet, anyway.

"Be with you in just a second, Miss Bertha. I need to put the *Oxford Advanced Learner's Dictionary* on hold for Laurence George down at the bookstore." Emma Kramer, the young librarian, smiled.

"Why does a bookstore owner need to check out a library book?" Bertha pushed a lock of damp hair back under her straw hat. That George man was another person she had a hard time liking. Such a pompous rascal!

There was a loud crash from the children's section and Bertha watched two young mothers struggling to pick up a puppet display that their toddlers had managed to knock down. Bertha shook her head in disgust. What was wrong with parents today? Her own mother would never have allowed Bertha or her brother to climb on the sofa and pull things from the shelf. Bertha sighed for the days when children were seen and not heard.

Jane rushed to help the flustered mothers set the puppets back in order and Bertha snorted. Let them clean up their own mess. Not for the first time, Bertha was glad that she had never had children of her own.

Her mind was called back to the task at hand by the bright voice of Emma Kramer.

"Okay, Miss Bertha, I think the *Oxford* is safely on hold. How can I help you?"

Bertha leaned against the circulation desk. Did the room look hazy or were her glasses just dirty? It took her a minute to focus on Emma's face.

"Here, let me find you a place to sit." Emma moved toward a wooden armchair. "Not the most comfortable seat in the house, but you can at least get off your feet for a few moments."

"Thank you, but I don't need a chair," Bertha snapped. Her vision was becoming clearer now. Just one of the flukes of old age, she surmised. One day it's your vision and the next it's your balance. She regained her composure and continued. "I just want to go down to the vault—you know, our Brubaker family vault."

Emma drummed her fingers on the circulation desk. "The vault? That old contraption in the library basement? No one has opened that for years. We don't even have the combination."

Bertha bristled. "Why would you even remotely feel the need to know the combination? That's my family's vault, and no one but a Brubaker has the right to open it."

Emma bit her lip to hold back a grin. "The last time I was down there was back in January. A couple of kids and I took the holiday decorations back to their storage bins. I just remember a musty smell and a lot of spiders. I'm sorry, Miss Bertha, but we can't allow patrons to go down to the basement."

Bertha placed her hands on the desk as she leaned close to Emma. Her chin quivered but her voice was firm. "Young lady, you hear me, and you hear me well. My family owned this building long before your grandparents were even born. Patrons? I would consider an *original* Brubaker quite a bit more than a patron!" The old lady was working herself into a fury. "You are not going to tell me what I can and can't do in my own building." She started to walk toward the basement door.

Emma stood up, nonplussed. "Tell you what," she said. "I'll make a compromise. I'll allow you to walk down to the vault, but if you aren't back in fifteen minutes, I'm coming down to look for you."

Bertha pursed her lips and drew herself up to her full five feet two inches. "Well," she said, shaking her head, "if she were alive, your mother would be appalled at your pushy ways. She knew her place. *She* was a real lady."

"That she was," agreed Emma, standing up and gesturing for Bertha to follow. Emma opened the door and stood aside as Bertha slowly descended underground.

The steps were steep and Bertha clung to the metal pipe that served as a railing. At the bottom, she leaned against a filing cabinet near the vault door to catch her breath. Maybe there was something to be said for clean, bright bank safes. Maybe she should consider moving the contents of the vault to a more accessible place. She wiped a cobweb away from the vault handle and took a small leather book from her tote bag. She squinted in the dim light as the old tumblers fell into place. She braced herself, and with all her strength pulled the lever. The vault door creaked open.

Piles of boxes and filing cabinets lined the walls of the vault, and for a brief moment, Bertha was discouraged. What were the odds of finding what she was looking for before that nosy Kramer girl came down looking for her? But the thought of the lives that would change from her discovery gave her a boost of energy and she opened a dusty box marked "Records." Inside, she sorted through old land records, financial reports, and birth certificates. Oh yes, birth certificates. Exactly what she was looking for. And she found it with her first try. It must be a sign that she was doing the right thing.

Of course she was doing the right thing.

Emma looked at her watch. Almost closing time. Except for her ordeal with Miss Bertha Brubaker, the day had gone fairly well. The Jacobs twins had continued to wreak havoc in the children's department until their exhausted mother finally carted them off, one under each arm. Emma glanced out the bubbled glass window beside her cluttered desk and looked toward the mountains framed by two spreading maples.

A small freckled boy grinned and waved as he walked past. Emma smiled and waved back. Was that Samuel, Sissy Lambert's youngest? She really had to do better with names. Folks could excuse the library's Friends group for forgetting people, but they were all a lot older than her mere twenty-seven years. They could get away with a few memory lapses.

A swirl of turquoise caught her attention and her gaze shifted to a slender woman in a long skirt disappearing around the corner by the old drugstore. Emma pushed a dark brown curl away from her face and squinted. The stranger's peculiar shade of red hair reminded her of someone she had known a long time ago. A coincidence, of course. She had tied up the past with a neat little bow and placed it safely in the back of her mind. There was no reason for old memories to reappear on this mild May morning. She had too much to do in the present to spend time brooding. She'd done her penance.

Emma turned her attention to the two dedicated volunteers who had stayed to help close.

"Time to call it a day, Marguerite. Jane. You've done a marvelous job—as usual!" Emma stood up and smoothed the wrinkles from her denim skirt. Although the Friends of the Library had never mentioned it, she knew that they wished she would take more care with her appearance. Or at least wear dress clothes. But Emma had always gone for comfort over style, and denim was an old friend. At least it was a skirt instead of jeans today.

"Just look at this mess!" Marguerite White sighed as she pulled a haphazard stack of magazines from the rack and began to arrange them into a neat pile. She paused to peer at Emma over her spectacles. Her long fingers plucked at the collar of her neatly pressed linen blouse. Marguerite dressed as though she were still working in security at Langley during the Vietnam years. Her height and regal stance belied her age. Though now in her seventies, most people assumed she was ten years younger.

Emma tucked the hem of her white cotton blouse into the waistband of her skirt. Marguerite always made her feel self-conscious.

Jane Allman smiled as she pushed an empty book cart back for another load of DVDs to shelve. "You know they'll just mess them up again tomorrow, Marguerite." Jane was fifty-nine, but her short hair was only now beginning to show strands of gray, and her face was still unlined. With the patience of Job, she took life for what it was: messy, irregular, and unpredictable. Even thirty years of teaching high school science hadn't jaded her cheery outlook.

"Well, ladies, I, for one, am ready to call it a day!" Emma twisted her long brown hair into a makeshift knot at the back of her neck. She had once thought a librarian's job was to order, catalogue, and shelve books. That classic description failed to mention the additional tasks required of a small-town librarian. She was also the interior decorator, publicity manager, library Friends director, maintenance person, and she performed a dozen other tasks too numerous to mention. She often clocked over fifty hours a week.

Emma yawned. Tonight she was looking forward to curling up in her recliner with an old, well-loved copy of her favorite novel, *Pride and Prejudice*. Her sister-in-law, Shirley, had cross-stitched one of the quotes from the book, and Emma had hung it over her reading chair: "I declare after all there is no enjoyment like reading! How much sooner one tires of any thing than of a book!" Somehow, having Jane Austen's own words hanging in her living room made Emma feel closer to the eighteenth-century novelist. It probably also showed the whole world what a nerd she was, she reflected as she gathered her purse and keys.

As if the universe decided to respond to Emma's evening plans with a counteroffer, the large mahogany doors swung open and two men entered. Emma stiffened. Of all the people who could possibly come barging into the library after closing hours, town manager Billy Brubaker was the last person she wanted to see. A well-dressed stranger walked slightly behind Billy and appeared to be surveying the bookshelves with unusual interest.

"Why, Miss Emma! How lucky we are to see your pretty face this evening! I was afraid you'd have locked up by now." Billy gave her a toothy smile and extended a pudgy hand. As usual, his dress shirt was wrinkled and his tie askew. Emma's eyes narrowed and she tried not to recoil as he took her hand in his clammy grasp.

"Well, Billy, we are, in fact, already closed," said Emma, glancing at the clock.

"You can't close with these charming ladies still here." He grinned at Marguerite and Jane and stepped behind Emma to put an arm around each.

"My faithful volunteers," said Emma. "They're just leaving. Since we're closed."

The women disentangled themselves from Billy's arms. Marguerite glared at both men, and Jane gave Emma a sympathetic glance.

"Don't forget, dear. The library Friends want you to join us for dinner Tuesday, a week from tomorrow. We're meeting at my house. Salmon croquettes."

"I wouldn't miss a meal prepared by our town's most famous chef," said Emma. She was grateful for Jane's attempt to intervene in the awkward intrusion. "Thanks, ladies. See you both tomorrow." Emma waved as they headed out the door.

Stifling a sigh, she turned back toward Billy with a pointed look.

"Oh, pardon my manners," sputtered Billy. "Allow me to introduce you to Mr. Jarrod Harmon. Jarrod, this is Emma Kramer, our library director."

The stranger, who had not yet said a word, stepped up to shake Emma's hand.

"Ma'am, pleased to meet you. Nice old place you have here." His eyes seemed to take in a swarm of dust particles swirling in the late afternoon sunlight. He handed her a smooth business card. *Jarrod Harmon, Resident Engineer, Department of Transportation.*

Emma looked at the card and then stared at her visitor in silence.

Mr. Harmon cleared his throat. "We'll try to make this quick. Actually, this is official business."

"Why so formal, Jarrod, my boy? We're all friends here!" Billy clapped him on the back and laughed, though Emma could see that he was uneasy.

Just then, the church chimes struck the quarter hour. "How about them bells, Harmon? Pretty nice, huh?" Billy grinned and ran his fingers through his hair.

"Nice," Mr. Harmon agreed, flipping through the pages of a yellow legal pad.

"Actually, according to my Uncle Albert," said Emma, becoming animated. "Those are the Westminster Quarters. The number of chime sets matches the number of quarter hours that have passed. The idea originated in Great St. Mary's, the university church in Cambridge. That's in England, by the way, Mr. Harmon." Emma couldn't resist the urge to put this stuffed shirt in his place.

Mr. Harmon continued to shuffle the papers in his hand. "All quite interesting, I'm sure, but as your bells tell us, it is now fifteen minutes past the hour, and I'm sure you want to get on with this conversation so you can go home."

"Shall we sit down?" Emma pulled some chairs away from the computers and the three sat facing one another across the worn Oriental carpet.

Mr. Harmon pulled out a thin black pen and began to tap it against the clipboard in his lap.

"Is there something wrong?" Emma looked from one man to the other. "Will someone please explain to me what this after-hours visit is about?"

"The good news is," Mr. Harmon began, "the Department of Transportation has agreed to fund a new highway to connect your little town to the rest of the world."

"That's the good news?" Emma arched her eyebrows. "I'm not overly excited to hear the bad news."

Mr. Harmon relaxed his face into a smile and leaned toward Emma. "Surely you can't be happy watching those sidewalks get tucked away so early. I think a major road would give this place a new lease on life. A new spark of enthusiasm."

"I rather like life as it is. That's why I choose to live here."

"Oh, you mean you weren't born here?"

She felt a flash of embarrassment. "I can't possibly see what my birth has to do with your so-called official visit."

"You're right. I apologize. Well, this construction will have an effect on you and your building here."

He pulled a multicolored map from his clipboard, and smoothed it across his lap.

"Here's the proposed path the highway will take: right past the Spare Change Diner, by the Bard's Nest bookstore, and . . ." His finger stopped tracing the red line.

"It's going right through the library!" Emma felt her heart flutter as if she had just gulped an espresso. "How can you even think of building this road? The library is in its path!"

Billy had been silent as Mr. Harmon unfolded the map, and he now shifted his weight on the creaky wooden chair, an I-told-you-so smirk on his face.

"Ma'am, this road is good for area landowners," Mr. Harmon replied. "It will bring more commerce to the area. More tourism. A chance for farmers to get some good prices for their land." The man's tone had changed and he said the words slowly and carefully, as if talking to a young child.

"Surely the Custer's Mill folks will be involved in this decision," said Emma, struggling to control her rising anger. "You *are* planning hearings on this proposal?" Her blue eyes blazed as she looked at his passive face.

"Yes, ma'am, the highway department always has hearings for this type of project. I'll be in Custer's Mill in a few weeks for the first of two hearings. We won't make a final decision until July. But we hope you'll consider supporting our proposal. With your buy-in we know others in town will get on board."

"Gentlemen, I must ask you to leave the library now," said Emma, standing up and walking to the door. "We're closed, and I need some time to digest this news. Good evening, Mr. Harmon. Billy."

The two men stood up and Mr. Harmon fastened the documents back into the clipboard. "We'll talk more later," he said, holding out his hand, then dropping it when he saw Emma's expression. "We'll try to come before closing hours next time."

As Emma held the door open for the men, a gust of wind swirled into the library, causing the notices on the bulletin board to flutter and flap. Clouds were forming in the west. A thunderstorm was brewing.

Chapter 2

Mill County Detective Jake Preston tossed a wad of paper toward the garbage can near the door. The paper swirled around the rim, ricocheted off the wall and fell to the floor. With a sigh, he got up to throw the scrunched document into the trash. The metaphor was clear: he'd missed the target once again.

He glanced down at the yellowed clipping from the *Winchester Star*. His wife, Mirabelle, had kept it inside her Bible for years. "Woman Killed in Fire." Kath Porter had been what – eighteen at the time? Her daughter, Mirabelle, had been two. The fire had been treated as a straightforward case – a stray firecracker had ignited, causing the blaze.

It wasn't until many months later that the issue of race had come up. Apparently some ambitious attorney had seen dollar signs and had tried to get the girl's mother to sue the town for a racially motivated crime. Ruth Porter was too smart to take him up on the offer, though. That bit of information he had found tucked into the corner of the local section of the June 1986 edition of the *Custer's Mill Times*—almost a year after the fire that had killed his mother-in-law.

Jake leaned back in his chair and surveyed the view from his window. Mirabelle had been right. It was gorgeous here in the heart of the Shenandoah Valley. Especially in late spring. The pink dogwood was in full bloom and the scent of lilac wafted through his open window. If only Mirabelle were here to enjoy it with him.

The jangling telephone brought him out of his reverie. It was probably Custer's Mill police chief, Pete Anderson. Pete was supposed to meet up with him before Jake picked up his daughter from the library this afternoon.

He put the aging newspaper back into a folder and reached for the phone.

The late afternoon sun was just beginning to send its rays through the southwestern library window. Emma looked up from her computer and stretched her hands over her head. The peal of the old reliable Westminster chimes told her that it was the quarter hour—the quarter hour of what, she wasn't sure. Emma was always amazed at how quickly a day could disappear when there was a lot to do. She stretched toward the ceiling and rotated her neck from side to side. She could sure use a lap or two around the track.

"What happens if I spill water on it?" A little girl stood at the checkout counter clutching a worn copy of *The Secret Garden*. She gave Emma a sidelong glance before her grey eyes focused on the wide planks of the floor.

"Maybe you shouldn't read it in the bathtub!" Emma smiled.

The little girl looked incredulous. "I can't read chapter books yet!" Emma's remark about reading in the bathtub was ignored, and she got the impression the child thought the statement too silly for comment. A shimmer of silver caught Emma's attention and her eyes were drawn to the pendant around the girl's neck. It was an intricately designed piece shaped into a circle with points radiating from its center.

Emma smiled, "Oh, will your mom read it to you then? It's a wonderful book—lots of secrets and hidden gardens."

"My mom is dead."

"Oh, I'm sorry. So is mine."

"Hmmm." The child shook her head and gave Emma the kind of look a parent gives a naughty toddler.

I'm striking out here, thought Emma as she scanned the book and handed it to the little girl who carefully tucked it into her grungy pink backpack. She pushed a lock of dirty blond hair out of her eyes.

"I reckon my dad might read it to me. But what happens if we spill something on the pages? Do we have to pay for it? I don't get an allowance, so if we have to pay for it, I won't read it." She scowled at Emma as if daring her to try to pry a penny from her tightly closed fingers.

"My dad's a policeman. We just moved here," she added, as if this bit of information would clear up any questions one might have about the family's economic situation. "You know, Jake Preston."

Emma vaguely remembered hearing one of the library ladies talking about the new county detective who'd moved to town recently. "Well, I'm glad to see you've already got a library card! And welcome to Custer's Mill. I hope you and your dad will like it here."

The girl shrugged and appeared unimpressed. "Maybe. But I don't have an allowance, anyhow."

Emma surveyed the library. There were only two young patrons left at the computers, and volunteer Nanette Steele was sorting books in the storage room, although for Nanette, sorting was more like throwing. She wasn't the most patient person, except when it came to her sheep and alpacas.

The clock hands were already pointing to five and Emma had plans to drive out to her dad's farm right after work. She returned her gaze to the little girl standing in front of her desk. The child couldn't be more than six or seven years old.

"Tell you what," Emma said, lowering her voice in a conspiratorial manner. "I'll make you a deal if you'll do a favor for me." She added in a whisper, "I might even pay for your book if you mess it up."

The girl's expression turned cautiously hopeful. "Yeah? What do you want me to do?"

"First of all, I need to know your name."

The girl shook her head as if chiding a troublesome child. "Didn't you see it when I checked out my book? My library card says, 'Kate Preston.'"

"You're absolutely right, Kate Preston! I completely forgot to look at your card."

"Can't you get in trouble for not knowing who you give books to?"

"Probably," Emma smiled. "But the computer knows that you checked out the book. We still have a record even if I am a forgetful librarian!" The young girl considered her doubtfully and Emma motioned for Kate to come closer. "Now, Kate, I have a job for you. See those people over at the computer? The two girls? Will you walk over and tell them that we close in five minutes?"

"Okay. They're my babysitters, Ali and Kirsten." Kate headed in the direction of the girls. Emma wondered if she would trust a couple of middle schoolers to watch over a young child. Then again, if there was no mom in the picture, it might be difficult to find reliable child care, especially if you'd recently moved into town.

She was being unorthodox, making deals with scruffy little waifs, but there was something about the child that reminded her of herself at the same age—back when the possibilities were endless, and the next adventure was as close as a new library book.

"They said okay."

Emma smiled. "Thank you so much, Kate. And Kate," she added as an afterthought, "if your dad doesn't have time to read to you, maybe you could come back here and we could read together."

Kate grinned and hoisted her book bag onto her small shoulders. Emma heard the girls mutter something about "drama" as they closed out the computer window. Their long ponytails swung with indignation as they pushed their chairs in.

"Can't go until Mr. Preston answers our text," said Ali as she pulled her phone from her small bag. Both babysitters turned and looked at Emma, simultaneously rolling their eyes at such a childish obligation. "He actually times us from the minute he texts us back until we tell him we're home. If we're a minute late he goes all crazy."

Emma was secretly impressed with Kate's dad's sense of responsibility. Chalk one up for the detective, she thought.

"I'll just lock the door so nobody else comes in, and we can wait until you hear back from Kate's dad."

As Emma turned the key in the old-fashioned lock, she admired the intricate etching along the perimeter of the dark mahogany doors. Pure craftsmanship. The entire library was an image of days gone by. From the carefully patched plaster walls to the rich, dark polished chair railing, the building spoke of careful attention to detail. Yes, this building must be saved. Emma intended to see that it was.

"Yoo-hoo! Anybody home?"

Drat! She had forgotten to lock the back door. *That* voice was not one she was particularly glad to hear. Pete Anderson, the town police chief. Emma could hear Nanette's groan all the way from the storage room. The sheep farmer and the local police chief had never been on amicable terms.

"Well, Lady Emma, how wonderful it is to see you!" Pete Anderson wasn't a huge man, but his sturdy, almost square form coupled with his booming voice seemed to fill up a room in a hurry. Before Emma had time to answer, her gaze was drawn to another man in uniform, one standing slightly behind Chief Anderson. Pete laughed and stepped aside. "Allow me to introduce a new member of the Thin Blue Line: Detective Jake—"

"Daddy!" Kate Preston pushed past Emma and ran into the newcomer's arms. He picked her up and carefully adjusted her small body on the hip that wasn't carrying the holster. "Daddy, this is my friend, Miss Emma. She let me borrow a book and said she would read it to me!"

"Wow, that's really nice." He smiled and nodded at Emma. Jake Preston was definitely the most handsome man she had seen in a while. He had the rugged, tanned look of a man who spent a lot of time outdoors, but his light brown hair streaked with blond gave him a slightly boyish appearance. Emma found the contrast quite attractive.

"I assume you are the accommodating librarian?"

Emma nodded, trying not to notice the deep dimple that danced just above the detective's left jaw.

"Hey, I was about to introduce you when this tornado came through!" Chief Anderson rubbed Kate's head and tangled her already messy hair.

"Ouch!" Kate glared at the offender. "You hurt my hair!"

"No worries!" Jake gently lowered Kate to the floor and stretched out his hand. "Pleased to meet you, ma'am."

Emma felt her heart skip a beat and was immediately annoyed at her reaction to this tall, good-looking man. He couldn't be over thirty, and yet he was widowed. She wondered what had happened to his wife, and how recently she had died.

"Wait a minute, Daddy. Why are you here? Kirsten and Ali just texted you. They were supposed to walk me home."

"Chief Anderson wanted to introduce me to Miss Emma, so I decided to just pick you and the girls up. Does that fit into your busy schedule, ma'am?" Jake gave a mock bow.

"You're silly, Daddy!"

Emma smiled. Will this man's superpowers never end? This new detective was not only incredibly attractive, but he also seemed to be a caring, attentive father.

"Well, Emma, I'm happy to meet you. The way my Kate likes books, I'm sure we'll be seeing a lot of you and the library."

Against her better judgment, Emma hoped this would be the case.

Chapter 3

The library Friends meeting had lasted later than she'd anticipated. Bertha adjusted her tote bag on her shoulder and tried to increase her pace up the short hill on Rosemary Street. She really should have let Jane drive her home. Not just because she was tired, but also because she had to get ready for the two guests she'd invited over that afternoon. Everything had to be just right—the food, the atmosphere and the timing. Yes, timing was everything. These two—her nephew, Billy, and her lawyer, Paul Stewart, had to be the first to know. After today, she could tell the entire town of Custer's Mill about her discovery. She smiled at the thought of the joy her news would bring to some. But of course her announcement wouldn't please everyone. In fact, there would be at least one person who would not be happy at all—one person whose life would change, and not necessarily for the better.

She pulled out a handkerchief to wipe the sweat from her face. Stopping to catch her breath, she admired the view of her ancestral home. It was over 150 years old, but still looked magnificent with its large rectangular windows symmetrically placed along the brick facing, and the two-story white columns flanking each side of the wide porch. The gardens that surrounded the manor house were especially beautiful in the late spring. Well-trimmed boxwoods and other shrubbery outlined the expansive gardens. Along the walkways, purple iris, red and yellow columbine, and pink snapdragons added bursts of color to the manicured landscape. Her favorite flowers, though, were the peach and apricot roses near the large maple tree.

Suddenly, the scent of roses was replaced by a slight whiff of sandalwood. "Daddy?" A tall form loomed in the shadow of the magnolia tree. "Daddy? Is that you?" The man began to sing, "Sweet Bertha girl, sweet Bertha girl, I want to dance with you!"

"Daddy! It is you!" Bertha struggled to hurry her pace, but when she got to the tree, the singing had stopped and the shadow had vanished. She shook her head. Of course it wasn't her father. He had been dead over forty years. What was wrong with her?

Bertha continued up the garden pathway, shaken from her experience. She saw Hiram trimming the hedge of boxwoods. Had he seen her father? No, he couldn't have. Her father hadn't been there. She straightened her hat and struggled to pull a note of authority back into her voice.

"I saw you working in the garden yesterday. You know I don't approve of you working on Sundays."

"Flowers don't know a Sunday from a Monday, Miss Brubaker." Although Hiram could quote the Bible as well as any divinity student, he didn't often attend church. The few times he graced the door of a house of worship, he had ended up in a heated debate with the minister over some minor theological point.

"Hiram, you've managed to cut yourself again on those thorns. I've told you countless times to wear gloves when you work with the roses. In fact, I just bought a new pair for you a week ago. Why aren't you wearing them?" Bertha frowned.

Hiram rose to his feet and looked Bertha squarely in the eye.

"Miss Brubaker, you pay me to keep this garden, and that is what I do. I must work the works of him that sent me, while it is day: the night cometh, when no man can work."

Bertha sighed. "Do you know the whole King James Bible by heart? Well, no mind. I won't have you bleeding all over the place. Come on in and get that cut bandaged."

"I'll take care of it all in good time." Hiram returned to pruning the roses as Bertha walked up the front porch steps.

The familiar smell of old wood greeted her as she entered the hallway and placed her hat on the side table. She glanced at the grandfather clock in the parlor. Already twelve thirty. Every bone in her body ached and she longed to lie down. Her head was throbbing but there was no time for self-indulgence, no time to process the strange encounter in the garden.

20

She took the Royal Doulton tea service from the china cupboard and spread it on the table. The set was her mother's, a true Southern belle. Their house had always been full of merriment, and oh, the parties they hosted! Girls in taffeta gowns flirting with dapper young men, maids dressed in crisp black and white flitting among the guests with their offerings of fine food, laughter drifting down the winding staircase to fill the rooms. Bertha shook her head and brought herself back to the present. Why was her mind drifting so much today?

By a quarter of two, everything was in place. Bertha looked around, and nodded her head in satisfaction. Now, if Billy just came on time.

She needn't have worried. At precisely two o'clock, the front door opened.

"Anybody home? Aunt Bertha?" Loud footsteps echoed on the parquet floor.

"Hello, Billy." Bertha inclined her head slightly for Billy to kiss her cheek. She tried not to wince as his rough, unshaven chin graced her face. "Come on in to the parlor."

Billy scooted a heavy wing-backed chair back from the table and reached for a teacake. "Nobody makes teacakes like you, Aunt Bertha. You are the best!" His enormous hand almost demolished the tiny dessert before it reached his mouth. Several crumbs had already collected on his shirt.

Bertha poured the tea and watched Billy devour the delicate sweets. It was a good thing she had saved some back in the kitchen or Paul Stewart would have to go without.

"Man, you ought to open a bakery with these teacakes, Aunt Bertha! They're the best I've had since the last time I ate with you!"

Bertha sighed. It would be nice just to sit here with Billy and watch him enjoy her baking, but there was pressing business at hand, and she must get on with it. She cleared her throat.

"Billy, I have called you here today to share something with you. I am hoping that when I'm finished you'll understand and feel as I do. As you know, a family as old as ours couldn't have existed without some secrets—things our forebears hoped would remain buried with them."

Bertha paused for a moment, to see if Billy was paying attention. It was difficult to tell. He seemed almost completely focused on consuming the desserts.

"You know that your father was my only sibling, and as his heir, you stand to inherit the family estate." Billy stopped, teacake poised in midair. She had his attention now.

"Well, yes, Aunt Bertha, I assumed I would take over the family money and lands, but not until it was time, um . . . not until you had passed, that is."

Bertha reached for the envelope in front of her. Her hands were shaking and she felt light-headed. She carefully took the letter from inside, unfolded the yellowed paper, and handed it to Billy.

"This was written by my father, your grandfather. There are documents to support what he says in this letter. It is time to bring this information to light. I have reason to believe that this will change the lives of several people in this community. But we're bound by our ancestors to do what is right—to honor my father's request."

Bertha watched as Billy read and reread the letter. His face registered an array of emotions: disbelief, anger, disgust.

"What a joke. You expect me to believe this? But his hands trembled as he folded the letter and placed it back in the envelope. "You said there is proof . . . what proof? Before I believe anything this crazy, I need to see some proof."

"Billy, let me remind you that I'm still the head of this family. I control the Brubaker estate and assets. Besides, none of this concerns you, really, until I'm no longer on this earth." Bertha could play this game, too. She sat with her back straight despite her throbbing head, and glared at Billy. She wasn't about to let him get the upper hand in this matter. "I haven't known about it myself for very long. I've done some checking, however, and there are official documents supporting the facts my father addresses. I've reviewed these documents myself. I thought it only fair to share this information with you." Bertha shifted in her chair as if a change in her position would help lessen the growing tension between them.

"Does anyone else know about this?" Billy asked.

"Well, my lawyer, of course." Bertha picked up a delicate china cup and took a sip of tea. Receiving no verbal response from Billy, she continued, "I'm sure you'll agree that we should do all we can to right the great wrongs that have been done. You understand that this information has resulted in a change in my will."

Billy stood up. "There's gotta be some mistake! One simple letter can't be that important—one little handwritten note shouldn't have the power to change my life this way! I have to get out of this stuffy room. I need some fresh air." He stumbled into the hallway.

"Before you go, Billy, there is one more thing I need to ask you."

Billy stopped, but didn't turn around.

"I couldn't help but notice that you have had some substantial amounts of money drawn from your trust. Not just once or twice, but on a regular basis. Is there something I should know about?"

Billy jerked his head up. "What? What do you mean by prying into my personal business? Who gave you permission? You have no right to dig through my personal records!"

Bertha reached out a hand, but he pushed it away. Shaken, she replied, "I am still executor of the estate. I receive financial records every year. I had not looked at them closely until last week. Paul Stewart is a good account manager, and I had no reason to double-check him. And I still trust him. I am just confused about your withdrawals. That's all."

Billy turned on his heels and headed toward the entryway.

Bertha called after him, but the wooden door slammed shut. From the parlor window, she watched as he banged his vehicle door and revved up the engine. He'd reacted worse than she had figured. Still, she knew she was in the right. She was just glad she'd lived long enough to set matters right.

She heard water running in the kitchen. So Hiram was finally taking care of that cut. She wondered how much he had overheard.

By the time Bertha cleared the remains of the tea and carried the empty plates to the kitchen, Hiram was nowhere to be seen. She filled the serving tray with a fresh supply of teacakes and made her way back to the parlor. This day was turning out to be more of an emotional strain than she had anticipated.

Billy turned off the engine and sat in his driveway, hunched over the steering wheel. His yellow cat jumped onto the hood of the car, meowing its displeasure at his master's delay in entering the house. Billy's thoughts tripped over each other as they scrambled to form into coherent ideas. Not once in his forty-five years had life been fair. From boyhood on, he had battled with some demon or other. First it had been his weight. "Billy's belly jiggles like jelly!" He could still hear the taunts of his classmates. His one hope had been to eventually become the wealthiest man in Custer's Mill, but two failed businesses and never-ending debt had held him back all these years. As soon as he inherited the Brubaker estate, he'd have the power that comes with wealth. But now, he wasn't so sure. Thanks to Aunt Bertha, that was all up in the air. He should have known the dream was too good to come true. There were only so many ways to slice a pie.

He pulled his cell phone from the inside pocket of his jacket and punched in the familiar numbers. He tapped the fingers of his free hand against the steering wheel. Come on. Answer! The conversation was going to be bad enough. The wait made it worse. Three. Four. Five. He'd give it one more ring.

"What do you want?" The voice on the other end of the line sounded irritated.

"I don't want anything." Billy passed a hand over his damp forehead. He had to stay calm. Later, he could scream at the heavens for the unfairness of it all. But right now, he had to keep focused. "There's just something you need to know."

"Well? Am I supposed to read your mind? Just spit it out. I'm in a hurry."

"You know that big windfall I was counting on? Well, it's not gonna happen." Billy squeezed his eyes tight. "And something else. She's found out about the money I've taken from the trust fund. She has her bloodhound of a lawyer on it."

There. It was all out now. Nothing he could do about it. Maybe this was a blessing in disguise. He waited for the stream of profanities to roll from the other end of the line, but the air was silent. Billy closed his phone and stared out into the evening sky. Somebody stop this train. He wanted off.

It was just after four o'clock when Bertha saw her lawyer, Paul Stewart, out the door. She was tired, but mostly satisfied by the turn of events. Old age had robbed her of a lot, but she was still able to control destinies, still able to chart the courses of others.

Bertha's head and back ached as she carried the tea tray to the sink. She'd almost forgotten that she'd invited Jane, Marguerite and Nanette over before the town meeting that evening. At least there were a few teacakes left for them. She certainly didn't have the energy to bake more. Although these ladies sometimes annoyed her, they were her dear friends. They deserved to know about her discovery before the rest of Custer's Mill found out.

And to add to it all, there was that whole business with the highway department. Did no one have a sense of history anymore? Tear down the library? That whole idea was absurd. Oh well. She would set things straight. She always did. The town of Custer's Mill had always relied on the Brubakers to make things right. She would not fail them. She was tired and emotionally drained, but she would not fail them.

If only she still had a servant or two living here. Washing up would have to wait until tomorrow, she thought with a twinge of guilt. She needed to lie down. After forty years she could still hear her mother's reproachful voice in the back of her mind. "Never leave for tomorrow what you can do today," the cool, cultured accent reproved. Well that was just it, she told the dutiful ghost. She couldn't do it today, and, besides, what did her mother know about any kind of manual labor? Ruth's mother, Elsie Porter, had always been there to do the cooking and the washing up. Both her mind and her body were drained. She had not anticipated how difficult it would be to carry out her mission. Bertha had always been known for her direct approach to life and its challenges, but this time she was forced to move carefully, cautiously, making sure events unfolded in the proper order. If she moved out of sequence, she didn't want to think about what might happen.

She rested her head on an ancient velvet pillow, a relic of days gone by. Her entire house—perhaps her entire life—was a relic, a vestige of an era past.

Since the passing of her parents four decades earlier, her life had shifted from the future to the past. She was no longer a Southern belle; she was simply Bertha Brubaker, aging spinster, keeper of the Brubaker estate and guardian of family secrets.

Her brother, William Jr., did not have much business sense, so Bertha had taken charge of the family's properties and investments and had managed them with great success. In her more uncharitable moments, Bertha felt hard pressed to name anything her brother had contributed to society, except perhaps producing a male heir to continue the Brubaker family name. There were some who would argue that her nephew, Billy, was less than an asset to the family and to the town. How he got to be hired as town manager was a pure mystery to her. Communication and people skills, she thought, were essential traits for a public administrator. Billy possessed neither. Now in his mid-forties, she doubted if he would even continue the family name. If only he could have found a suitable wife and raised a family of his own. If only.

Bertha's train of thought was interrupted by a strong scent of rose water. Her eyes opened wide as she glimpsed a shadow of a pale pink gown and her mother's familiar face behind the velvet settee. Her hand flew to her throat and she gasped, "Mother? Mother? Is that you?" A cool hand brushed over her brow and she heard a gentle voice say, "Time for bed, little one." Just then, the grandfather clock chimed the hour and Bertha jumped in her seat. The image and the perfumed air vanished, and Bertha struggled to regain her composure. What was wrong with her? Was she losing her mind? She sighed heavily. All things considered, it had been a profitable day, though. Old wrongs would soon be righted and justice would be served.

Just then, she heard a sharp knock at the door and sat up, startled, her heart pounding in her ears. Why did some people insist on rapping on that ancient doorknocker when there was a perfectly good, lighted doorbell in plain sight? She rose slowly and painfully from the recliner. Who could be calling now? She squinted one eye and peered through the stained-glass inset, then opened the door to a familiar face.

Chapter 4

The evening of the eagerly-awaited town meeting was unseasonably warm. The three elderly Custer's Mill Library Friends had started out walking at a brisk pace, but were forced to finish their journey at a slower tempo. Although the calendar said it was only the end of May, the humidity indicated otherwise. Most of the neatly manicured lawns along Rosemary Street were lush and green. Lawnmowers hummed here and there, and the air was filled with the fragrance of newly clipped grass.

"Tell me again why we're humoring her?" Nanette Steele adjusted her straw hat and looked at the small cluster of women walking beside her.

"We're not humoring her at all," Marguerite said, flicking a mosquito off Nanette's hat. "Bertha asked us to stop by her house for tea and cakes and we simply obliged. I, for one, am much too old to humor anybody."

"All in the semantics," grumbled Nanette. "Her Majesty summoned, and we, her loyal court jesters, are appearing at her doorstep."

"Ladies, please," said Jane, ever the peacemaker. She placed a hand on each of the opponent's shoulders. "There's really no need to squabble. We'll just stop by Bertha's house, eat a few cookies, and see what she has to tell us. We really can't stay long anyway; the public hearing is in thirty minutes."

"That's a joke. Public hearing, my foot!" Nanette found a perfectly round pebble and kicked it with the steel toe of her scuffed brown work boot. The stone made a beeline for the 1995 Lincoln lounging along the curb, missing the glossy finish by mere inches and landing with a clank against the custom chrome of the rear hubcap.

"Good thing the professor didn't see you! He loves that car." Marguerite looked up and down the street as if expecting to see Professor Albert Nelson storming toward them.

"Huh," snorted Nanette. "That musty fellow doesn't take his eyes off of his books long enough to notice anything. Has he given you the spiel about our library building having some kind of historical significance? He took up my entire morning yesterday going on and on about the research he is doing on some old buildings in the area. I'm sure I don't know what he's talking about!"

"Well, it is an old building," Marguerite replied. "Maybe he'll dig up something that will keep the place from being torn down because of that dreadful highway!"

"Dream on," said Nanette.

"We'll see." Jane shrugged. "Perhaps we should all just have a little faith."

Rosemary Street ended at the entrance to the Brubaker estate. The gate to Bertha's long drive stood open. A loud roar suddenly pierced the quiet air—a disjointed, growling sound that seemed to come from somewhere behind the house. Several frightened birds made hasty exits from the maple tree and a startled squirrel leapt from a fence post and ran frantically across the path. A rust-covered green van backed into the lane and barreled its way across the graveled space beside the garden cottage.

"Maniac!" yelled Nanette to the disappearing vehicle. "That man is going to kill somebody one day! They ought to take his license. He has no business driving his Green Hornet death wagon around like that!"

"Poor Hiram," sighed Jane. "He never did fit in, did he? Even in school he was a loner."

"A loony is more like it." Nanette craned her neck to watch the van turn rapidly onto Main Street without stopping. "I don't know why Bertha keeps him on as her gardener."

"I heard he has a green thumb," said Jane. "Reba Dove says he can make anything grow in any kind of soil."

"Green thumb or not, that man is crazy. Ought to be locked up."

The women made their way across a neatly maintained stone path, up the main walkway to the front porch, and stopped in a semicircle in front of the imposing door.

"You ring the bell, Marguerite. She likes you best." Jane urged her friend toward the door.

"Like?" snorted Nanette. "She doesn't like anybody!"

Marguerite stepped to the front of the group and rang the doorbell. There was no sound of stirring inside, and the women waited almost breathlessly to hear the slide of shuffling feet and the squeak of old hinges. Nanette pushed past Marguerite and hammered with the heavy door knocker.

"Open up the door! Anybody home?"

Her words echoed through the silent air and bounced back off the trees. There was still no sound from inside the house.

"Maybe she forgot she invited us over and already left for the town meeting." Jane looked anxiously at the drawn shades. The house had a vacant air about it.

"Why don't you try the door and see if it's locked?"

Nanette turned the knob and was surprised when the heavy door swung open.

"Come on, ladies! Let's get this show on the road!" She motioned for the others to follow.

The two women filed in behind Nanette. The hallway was dark and smelled of lavender. Ahead the women could see the parlor to the right and the dining room to the left. Before they could discuss which direction they should take, Nanette was already leading them into the parlor.

Even at first glance the room was striking. The walls were covered in deep scarlet wallpaper, and the same rich shade of red was mirrored in the heavy curtains that covered the wide bay windows. A collection of iron clocks decorated the mantel, and hanging above the fireplace itself was a beautiful quilt pieced together in an unusual rose pattern.

But the quilt was definitely not the focus of the group as their eyes scanned the room; for there, lying across the velvet settee, was Bertha Brubaker. She was dressed as usual in her impeccably tailored clothes, diamond brooch, and sapphire rings. Her face was covered with its customary layers of powder and rouge, but her eyes stared sightlessly up at the crystal chandelier.

It was obvious Bertha wasn't going anywhere, now or ever.

Chapter 5

Jake filled a pan with water and set it to heat on the range.

"Daddy?" Kate carefully replaced a gold crayon in the box and looked up at Jake with a disapproving frown on her face. "Daddy, are we having hot dogs again? We had hot dogs for supper last night. And my teacher says they're not good for you."

"Well, maybe your teacher would like to come and make us some supper then," said Jake, as he dumped three hot dogs into the water and placed a bowl of frozen mixed vegetables in the microwave.

"Let's ask her!" said Kate, jumping up from the table where books, pencils, and a pink backpack lay scattered.

"Right now, I'm asking you to clear off this table," said Jake. "We need some space to eat our hot dogs."

"The library lady says she trusts me with this book," Kate said as she held up the worn copy of *The Secret Garden,* then stacked her school supplies neatly on a chair. "She says if I mess it up or spill things on it, she'll pay for it. I told her I don't have an allowance and can't pay. She's nice. She asked if my mommy would read me the story, but I told her my mommy was dead," she added matter-of-factly, pushing her long, tangled hair out of her face and managing to add a few more tangles in the process. "I'm going to get ten books at the library every week."

Jake's jaw tightened as he looked at his daughter. As usual, anguish welled up whenever he had unexpected thoughts of Mirabelle. He treasured the moments when he could sit alone and choose to remember her—her smell, the way her long, curly hair always fell across her eyes when she turned the soil in her little flower bed, the gracefulness in her hands as she worked in the kitchen, her hand on his cheek as she'd

31

caress him for no special reason. She loved to make up goofy poems and she always said he was too serious for his own good. Mirabelle was his lighthearted alter ego.

Jake had moved to Winchester when he was twenty-one to work as a security guard and study criminal justice at the community college. He'd finished his training at the police academy just the week before they met. Mirabelle was in her third year studying violin at Shenandoah University. Eight months later they were married.

Kate was too young to have clear memories of her mother. She was only two years old when the call came—the call that told him his wife was dead, killed instantly when she fell asleep and her car rolled down an embankment on her way home from the community orchestra's final concert of the summer. The concert he was supposed to go to. He'd been working late at his job as police officer for the City of Winchester, and told her he was too tired that night. If he'd come with her, Mirabelle would still be alive. The wave of guilt washed over him like it always did. He felt his face flush.

Kate shook his arm insistently, turning Jake's attention abruptly to the present.

"Daddy! The water's spilling all over the stove!"

Jake quickly pulled the boiling pan of hot dogs off the burner, water sizzling and popping on the hot element. You'd think he could at least cook hot dogs without screwing it up. He sighed as he set out the buns and dished out the vegetables.

During the meal, Kate told him all the details about her trip to the library, and her happy chatter lifted Jake's somber mood. It was good to be here with Kate. A place that blended sad and happy memories. Although Mirabelle and her grandmother, Ruth, had moved to Winchester after the fire, Ruth had the house rebuilt. Mirabelle had often told him it held memories of many happy childhood weekends and holidays spent here with her grandmother.

He and Mirabelle had planned to move here and raise their family—four kids, a dog, and some chickens, that's what they'd dreamed of. He'd be a detective and she would teach violin. Well, at least part of the dream came true, he thought bitterly. He and Kate had arrived just a few weeks ago when he started a new job as detective for the Mill County

Police Department. He was determined to salvage as much joy as he could, for Kate's sake. And maybe for his own sake, too.

Chapter 6

Kate had been in bed for about an hour when the call came. Jake gave his daughter one last kiss and closed her bedroom door softly. *The Secret Garden* lay on the pillow beside her—she had insisted on sleeping with it. Two young teens watched him from the hallway, and he motioned for them to follow him into the living room. "Well, she's asleep, girls. Thanks for coming on such short notice. Think you'll be okay, Kirsten? Ali?"

"I think the two of us can handle a sleeping seven-year-old, Mr. Preston," Kirsten said. The girls exchanged a quick glance.

"I'm sure you can. I'm counting on it."

Jake knew the girls thought he was an overly fussy parent, an excessive worrier. But they were young. One day they'd understand the intensity of love and concern parents feel for their children. He hated leaving Kate at night. For the hundredth time he wondered if he'd made the right decision in accepting the detective job in Mill County. But the pay was good and it was high time he got away from Gordie Bosworth, his nemesis in the Winchester police department.

Jake's ability to focus on his work had helped him cope after Mirabelle died, and now it was time to turn his full attention to the call he'd received. He said a quick goodbye to the sitters and hurried to his squad car. Code Blue at the Brubaker mansion. Most likely it was Miss Brubaker herself. She was an old woman. Jake had answered this type of call many times up in Winchester. Still, he needed to show his new boss he knew how to handle this kind of investigation.

Two paramedics were leaning on the ambulance as Jake pulled into the driveway. He stepped out of the squad car and looked around for

Pete Anderson, but the Custer's Mill police chief was nowhere to be seen. Pete's junior officer, Jason Dove, was in uniform and sitting on the top porch step. He jumped to his feet and extended his hand as Jake approached. "Hello, sir. I'm Patrolman Dove. Chief Anderson isn't here, but I'll do what I can to assist you. It's an unattended death, sir."

"Miss Brubaker?"

Jason nodded.

"Thanks. Glad to meet you, Patrolman Dove," said Jake, returning a firm handshake. "Everything under control?"

"We're waiting on the medical examiner, sir." The young deputy pulled out a clipboard. "No signs of foul play—no broken windows or picked locks. I'd say she just died in her sleep." He stopped abruptly and blushed. "But of course I'm no expert."

Jake smiled and stepped around a shovel balanced against the railing. Nanette Steele was standing by the front door, hands on hips.

"About time the big boys showed up. Pete Anderson couldn't be bothered to come, I guess."

"Remind me again of your name please, ma'am." Jake's voice was polite but held an edge. It wasn't difficult to see who was in charge.

"Nanette Steele." Nanette raised her eyebrows slightly, but she stood aside and allowed Jake to enter the hallway. He scanned the hall, taking in two more women standing by. "I understand that you're the detective in charge here," Nanette's frank gray eyes met Jake's blue ones, unabashed, "but can you tell us where our renowned police chief is right now?"

"It's my job to ask the questions here, Miss Steele," said Jake. But perhaps he might be getting ready for that town meeting? The one about the proposed new highway?"

Nanette started. "The town meeting! We have to cancel! We can't have a meeting with Bertha lying in there. Marguerite, we have to call the town office. Tell Hoyt what has happened. I know it's late, but he'll understand."

Jake nodded to the women, and walked into the parlor. Bertha Brubaker was slumped down on the velvet settee. Her face was flushed a bright red, but her lips were outlined with a tinge of blue.

"So she was dead when you arrived?" Jake asked the remaining paramedic, who was snapping his case shut.

"Yes, sir. Still warm, though."

"Thanks, you can go now. I'll stay here and wait for the coroner."

The paramedic gave Jake a small salute and turned to go. He hesitated. "You know, sir, her lips don't look right to me . . . but I'm not the expert here."

As if on cue, a small black Ford pulled up in front of the house, and a tall, gray-haired man stepped out.

"Where'd he come from?" whispered Jane. "I thought I knew every handsome man in seven counties!"

"Hush, Jane!" Marguerite pushed her friend aside and extended her hand to the newcomer.

"Marguerite White. Thank you for coming so quickly. We—my friends and I—found the body. As you can imagine, it was quite a shock for us!"

"I was on call this weekend. Just doing my job." The man looked bewildered.

"But are you new to the area?" Jane sidled closer. "I don't remember seeing you around town."

Jake stepped out into the hallway and the man gave him a helpless look. Jake's eyes crinkled in amusement.

"I'm Jake Preston, the attending officer. I assume you're the medical examiner?"

"Justice Atkins. Pleased to meet you." The men shook hands and walked toward the parlor. Jake stopped suddenly and turned his attention back to the ladies. "Did I hear you say you found the body?"

"We did," replied Jane. "Bertha wanted us to stop by before the meeting. She said she had something to tell us. When we got here, she was ... gone."

"She said it was something important," said Nanette. "Of course, she always thought everything she said was important. You don't think someone killed her to shut her up, do you, with all this business about a road going through Custer's Mill?"

"Really, Nanette? There's not even a shred of logic in that statement," Marguerite shook her head.

Jake smiled. "I'm sure this has been quite a shock, ladies. Just stay in the hallway until I can get someone to formally take your statements."

Suddenly a commotion on the porch caught everyone's attention, and Billy Brubaker rushed wild-eyed into the room, followed by Patrolman Dove.

"Sorry, sir! He seems real upset, and I tried to calm him down but he ran right past me before I could grab him."

"It's all right, Jason. I'll talk to him." Jake watched Billy as he stood staring at his aunt's body, his hands clasped tightly together against his stomach. Jake had seen this reaction before. "Jason, get a large bowl or something from the kitchen. Fast."

Jake held out his hand and Billy grasped it like a lifeline. "I'm so sorry about your aunt."

Billy looked at Jake with a blank stare. "This can't be real. I just saw her earlier today! She made me my favorite teacakes. I think I'm going to be sick."

Jason pushed a large bowl into Billy's hands and the older man staggered into the hallway. Jake nodded for Jason to follow. Both men returned a few minutes later, Billy mopping his face with a handkerchief and looking pale and shaken.

"Mr. Brubaker, please sit down." Jake motioned toward an ornately carved wooden armchair, away from the settee where Dr. Atkins had begun his work. "What time did you have tea with your aunt?"

Billy ran his hands through his short hair as if trying to jog his memory. Two o'clock, I believe. Somewhere around then. Aunt Bertha wanted me to come by . . . she had some papers to show me." And then, as if he had a sudden revelation, he jumped to his feet and looked around the room, his eyes wide with alarm. "Where are they? What have you done with them?"

Jake raised his eyebrows. "Mr. Brubaker, please sit down. No one has removed anything from the room. We have to treat this like a crime scene since no one was here when she died. It's routine."

Billy's eyes widened. "A crime scene! She was an old lady. Nobody expected her to live forever!" He took a deep breath and tilted his head back, eyes closed. "Bless her dear old soul."

Loud whispers from the doorway caused Jake to turn his head. The three ladies stood on tiptoe, peering into the room. No doubt they were relishing their front-row seats to the present drama. Jake turned to Jason Dove. "Kindly escort these ladies to their homes, and tell them that we'll be taking their statements later this evening."

In the parlor, Billy sat in silence. The coroner was just finishing his initial examination.

"What do you think?" Jake nodded toward the body of Bertha Brubaker.

Dr. Atkins looked puzzled. "Seems pretty routine, but I want to take a few samples to send off to the state lab, just to be thorough. After I get what I need, I'll release the body to the family."

Billy stood up. "I'm planning to call Johnson's Funeral Home and get Bob over here as fast as I can. You're not going to mess with Aunt Bertha's body. There's absolutely no reason to…"

Dr. Atkins gave Billy an even stare. "Hold off on that call, Mr. Bruebaker. I'll let you know when I'm ready to release the body."

"That's ridiculous," said Billy. "Total foolishness. Waste of taxpayer money."

"Mr. Brubaker, please." Jake put a firm hand under Billy's elbow. "Come with me. I'd like you to leave now, and we'll talk later. Before you go, though, I'll need your cell and home phone numbers." Billy jerked his elbow away and his hands dropped to his side and stalked out of the room.

Dr. Atkins and Jake exchanged glances. "You just never know how relatives might react in these situations," said the doctor.

Minutes later, Billy lumbered out of the house, holding a hand to his forehead and walking with the stooped shuffle of an old man. But his white face began to redden in anger when he spotted Hiram Steinbacher working in the garden, digging weeds from a bed of brilliant blue campanula.

Hiram straightened and leaned on his hoe as Billy approached him.

"Hiram, go away. We don't need you here any longer."

Hiram stared at Billy in silence, a deep frown creasing his forehead.

"Put your tools away," Billy said. "My aunt may have tolerated you, but that's over. You're a loser, and I won't have losers on my property. Get out."

Hiram turned, carried his hoe to the nearby tool shed and placed it on its proper hook. Without comment, he walked to his green van. As it roared to life, he fixed Billy with a long, direct gaze. Billy stared, hands on hips until he saw the van turn and disappear from view on Rosemary Street. Then, his shoulders slumping once more, he walked to his car.

Jake stood near the boxwood hedge, where he had observed with interest the exchange between Billy and Hiram. He took a deep breath and exhaled slowly. It was a shame he hadn't been able to get to know Miss Brubaker before she died. She seemed like an interesting old lady. Probably a bit overbearing, but still ... He watched the paramedics load her body into the waiting ambulance.

"No use running the lights on this one," one of the men said as he closed the squad door.

"Appreciate it, man," said Jake, clapping the paramedic on the shoulder. "Thankless job, isn't it?"

Chapter 7

Jason Dove eased his squad car into the police station parking lot. Shep Crawford, one of the town's maintenance workers, leaned against the wall at the top of the outside steps, a plastic straw clenched in his mouth. As soon as he saw Jason, he turned and disappeared into the building. It was obvious Shep didn't like him. Maybe it was a grudge from the ancient past. Jason's grandma, Reba Dove, told him that back in high school, Shep had quite the crush on her. Maybe his heart got broken. Anyway, Shep had never married, and now he lived with his old granny out on a badland farm that barely grew enough vegetables to feed the two of them through the winter. He shrugged. Jason didn't intend to let Shep's misplaced jealousy ruin his day.

The police department was housed in the town's former high school, a brick federal-style building with the lovely architectural accents of bygone days. The town had never replaced the original large windows, so even after years of remodeling, it still looked like an old school, with high ceilings and concrete steps worn in the center from years of foot traffic.

It was after seven in the morning and the sun had already been up for an hour. The best part about night shift was watching the sun rise over the Blue Ridge, Jason thought. As far as he was concerned, there was no place prettier than the Shenandoah Valley. Not that he'd traveled much, but he loved the wide open pastureland that ended in forests and mountains, with countless amazing views that went on forever. It always made him glad. He never ceased to wonder at the stroke of good luck that had placed him right back at home as soon as he had graduated from the police academy. All of his buddies had told him that he would have to pay his dues somewhere in the poor section of a big city. That he couldn't possibly work in his small hometown of Custer's Mill right from the start. But they were wrong. Jason Dove was twenty-one years old and already had the job of his dreams.

He took the stairs two at a time. He'd file his timesheet and shift log before tackling his usual stack of pancakes and sausages at the Spare Change Diner. The small office he shared with two other officers was empty. He glanced at the bulletin board littered with notices and reminders, searching for the latest work schedule to see if he had to work next Friday night. He was hoping to ask Yvette Conrad out to a movie that night. Looked like the chief hadn't posted it yet.

The lone metal desk in the room was cluttered with a couple of coffee mugs and pen and paper clip holders. Notes and doodles covered the worn blotter. Jason pulled up a wooden chair and selected a form from one of the folders protruding from three gray metal upright dividers along the back of the desk. It was then that he heard voices talking inside the chief's office across the hall. The chief was in early today and it was impossible not to notice his deep voice.

Jason shifted his long legs in his chair, hoping the chief wouldn't come out and find him here, listening. He'd only been on the job for three months, and he intended to make a career of police work. It wouldn't do to have his boss finding fault with him in these early days.

"My problem is your problem too." The chief's visitor sounded angry. "I thought we understood each other."

Jason hurried to place his timesheet and log in the proper boxes, then gathered his lunch bag, eager to get away. He closed the office door quietly and turned, almost bumping head-to-head with Shep Crawford, who was leaning against the wall. Shep's sparse yellow-white hair was combed over in an unnatural part in an unsuccessful attempt at covering a growing bald spot. Two of Shep's tobacco-stained front teeth had noticeable chips, and his hazel eyes held a sly, animal-like squint.

"Quittin' time for you, Jason?" drawled Shep with a lazy grin.

"Yep. I'm about to buy me some breakfast. Beautiful morning, isn't it? Later, Shep."

The older man sneered. "Later," he mimicked.

Jason climbed into his jeep and started the engine, his mind drifting back to the snatches of conversation he'd overheard. Peculiar.

Wonder who that was with the chief? His stomach growled, and he put the car in gear. Within seconds, his thoughts had turned to the more immediate problem of whether to order sausage or bacon with his breakfast bonanza pancake stack.

Three members of the Friends of the Library were already at the diner when Jason pulled into his familiar parking spot. They had forgone their usual place at the counter and instead were huddled in a booth near the back of the restaurant.

"I thought she'd live forever," sighed Jane. "She seemed invincible."

"Well, as old Hiram would say, 'It is appointed unto every person to die.'" Nanette stirred two packs of artificial sweetener into her black coffee.

"I fear, Nanette, if you keep spooning that poison into your drinks, your 'appointed time' will come sooner rather than later." Marguerite picked up a flaky scone and began to spread it with butter.

"We've all gotta go sometime." Nanette sipped her coffee with relish. "But you're right, Jane. I didn't think she was in bad health either."

Marguerite looked skeptical. "Still, I suppose the heart can go without warning. I wonder if that new detective will let us pick out some decent clothes to bury her in. These young folks don't know how to match color with skin tone."

"She's dead, Marguerite. Just what do you expect her skin tone to be? Peach? Raspberry?" Nanette shook her head. "Still, I don't see why they wouldn't let us in the house to get her clothes. I'll call that Preston detective after a while."

Chapter 8

Three scoops per pot. The words were carefully scripted in flourishing letters, a relic of the days when penmanship was part of the regular school curriculum. Marguerite. Emma smiled. Nobody else she knew could make coffee instructions appear elegant. Still, three scoops rendered a mediocre pot of coffee, slightly weak and certainly not enough steam to get her through this Friday. No, today was more of a five-scoop day.

A sharp rap on the library door startled Emma and she let the measuring spoon fall with a clatter. Drat those impatient patrons! The sign clearly said, "Open at 10:00." Emma glanced at her watch. Almost nine thirty. The incessant knocking continued. Emma planted her feet more firmly in place. This person was going to have sore knuckles if he kept up the pounding for thirty minutes.

A sudden click and grating scrape were followed by a triumphal "Aha! Haven't lost my touch!" A petite, delicate-looking girl breezed into the foyer, past the circulation desk, and straight into Emma's office.

"Remember when we picked old Solomon's lock back in high school to get our test papers back before he graded them?"

Emma's jaw dropped. She must be hallucinating. This couldn't be ... but it was! Serafina Wimsey! The ginger-haired apparition she'd glimpsed three days ago had been real!

The intruder swept across the room and gave Emma an enormous hug. Serafina squeezed hard, not seeming to notice that Emma had stiffened and didn't return her embrace.

"Did you just break into the library?" Emma stepped back and surveyed the lovely creature in front of her. Long curls of copper-colored

43

hair trailed in a veil down her back. Turquoise eyes perfectly matched the flowing skirt that fell gracefully to meet slim ankles.

"We haven't seen each other for five years and all you can do is lecture me?" She gave Emma a mock hurt look. "I'm surprised you don't have your little spiral notebook out noting any changes in my appearance." Serafina wrinkled her nose. "Do you still play Harriet the Spy? I know you sure irritated a lot of the profs. at college with your little bouts of note taking!"

Emma's face was turning scarlet.

"Oh, lighten up, Kramer! I'm just teasing! Anyway, I need to fax this tea order before ten o'clock. Where's the fax machine?"

"Twenty-five cents a page," murmured Emma.

Serafina raised her eyebrows but said nothing.

Emma heard the back door open. Great. Marguerite and Nanette were coming in for their regular volunteer shifts—just the pair to stir the pot.

"A fair pickle he was in," Nanette was saying. "Thought he didn't get poison ivy, so he tackled that patch with both hands and feet!"

"Serves him right!" Marguerite shook her head. "Oh my goodness! Look who's here!"

"Nanny! Mags!" Serafina stopped punching numbers on the fax machine and ran to greet the two women.

No one in the entire world but Serafina Wimsey could get away with calling Marguerite White "Mags." But the nickname brought a bright smile to Marguerite's face. She gave Serafina a quick peck on the cheek and stood back to gaze at her. "It's been so long, dear. You look wonderful."

"Where've you been all these years, you little rascal?" said Nanette. "You go away to college in the big city and forget about all of your friends back in Custer's Mill. And for heaven's sake, child, why do you smell like garden dirt?" The old woman's voice was gruff, but it was easy to tell she was delighted to see Serafina.

"It's patchouli, silly! It's the latest thing! At least . . . in the city."

"Makes sense. City people who have never gotten soil under their fingernails wanting to smell like dirt!"

Serafina wrinkled her nose. "Anyway, I'm back! Gonna stick around for a while. Laurence is letting me rent the old flea market

44

building. I'm gonna open up a shop . . . a tea and herb shop! But I'll be working part time at the diner until it really takes off."

"One of those New Age nonsense places?" Nanette growled.

"Oh, you're such an old fogey!" Serafina patted Nanette's arm. "You should give herbs a try!"

"Oh, she gave 'herbs' a try," said Marguerite. "But that was back in the sixties and she almost got arrested!"

Emma stared at the flurry of activity around her. This could not be happening. It simply could not be happening. But there she was, in her charming, brilliantly colored glory, appearing out of nowhere like a leprechaun. Serafina, her former best friend, and now arch nemesis, was her only link with a past she'd rather forget.

Chapter 9

The Spare Change Diner and Grocery Store was many things to many people. To young parents, it was a place to pick up diapers without having to take the twenty-mile trek to the department store in Mill City. To working families, it was a place to buy TV dinners and frozen pizza as last-minute dinner solutions. To the small group of people sitting at the counter slurping strong black coffee, it was a regular Saturday morning gathering place. The Friends of the Library took up half the bar's counter space with their papers, folders, and three-ring binders.

"I think we can find enough ammunition to save our library." Jane Allman spoke with a note of confidence she didn't exactly feel. "But I sure wish Bertha were still here. She'd make sure we didn't lose the building to a super highway."

Laurence George, sole proprietor of the Bard's Nest bookstore, set his cup down with a thud. "If you ask me this town is going to hell with or without a handbasket; it doesn't have a mind of its own. The people think collectively, like sheep. Some slick-talking man in a business suit comes down from D.C. and tells them he'll give them a pretty penny for their farmland. They gawk at the gold on his finger and the Rolex on his wrist and fork over their inheritance for a pittance."

"You're preaching to the choir, Laurence." Nanette pushed an unruly curl out of her eyes and pulled out a notepad. "The library Friends have come up with ninety-five reasons the library building should not be torn down."

"You might have ninety-five reasons, but there ain't a single one would hold up in a court of law." The voice came from the far end of the counter of the Spare Change Diner. Shep Crawford spat a stream of brown liquid into a plastic bottle. "Ya'll don't know a good deal when it smacks you plumb in the face. Why I just got word from John Makepiece up in Fairfax that his boys are ready to offer top dollar for some of this empty farmland."

He spat again. "It ain't like we're running people off their property. Most of them are growing too old to keep up with farmin' life. What's wrong with a bunch of nice, young families moving into town?"

"Okay, Shep! That clears everything up then." Laurence feigned relief. "Just put that on the application. Just say, 'Only upwardly mobile young people need apply.' What if, say, an upwardly mobile, wealthy young gang boss decides to move in? Will his money work the same as your young executives' cash?"

Shep threw a handful of change down on the counter, slammed his chair against the bar, and walked out without answering.

"Sour grapes," murmured Jane.

"Oh, forget him. Don't waste your time." Nanette pounded her fist on the counter. "Let's get down to business. We have to come up with a unified message to take to the town meeting. I just wish . . ." her voice trailed off.

"Wish what?" asked Marguerite.

"Oh, just that Bertha would have been able to tell us what she knew about this whole business."

"You really think that old gossip knew anything worth sharing?" Pete Anderson strolled in, twirled a bar stool into place, and sat down. "Cuppa strong black tar, sweet stuff. Nice to see you back in town, Miss Wimsey." Pete grinned at the young woman behind the bar. Serafina glared as the police chief leaned over the counter and winked.

"Back off, buster. You're in my space." Serafina's voice was playful but her eyes were hard.

"Oooo—a little fire in that one!" Pete leered.

"Ironic that you should mention heat," said Serafina as she casually sloshed the pot of hot coffee so that several large splashes landed on Pete's shirt. "I'm so sorry, sir. Clumsy of me."

"Why you little—" sputtered Pete, jumping to his feet. I'll have you arrested! I'll . . ." He kicked a small wooden chair against the wall and one of the front legs clattered to the floor. "Get me a washcloth right this minute!" Pete's face had grown red and a large vein popped out on his neck.

"Oh, grab an ice cube and cool off," said Serafina as she tossed him a dishtowel and disappeared into the kitchen.

A soft snicker came from the group around the bar. Pete jerked his head to face them. They had stopped talking and were busying themselves with their coffee—stirring in sugar, adding cream, and pretending to warm their hands on the cooling mugs.

"What's so funny? Never see a police officer assaulted?"

"I thought you knew Serafina better than that," said Nanette, stifling a giggle.

Pete soaked up the coffee with the towel and threw the stained cloth across the bar. "I'll have her job before she knows what hit her!"

"So you're not going to be one of her customers at the tea shop?" Nanette winked at Pete.

"I'll see that place closed down if she keeps abusing police officers."

"You better hope they don't sue you for destruction of property!" said Laurence, glancing at the broken chair.

"That piece of junk?" Pete gave him a scornful glance. "By the way, what were you geezers gossiping about when I walked in? You sure shut up pretty quickly the minute you saw a badge."

"Library business," said Marguerite curtly. The group stared at him in silence.

"Well ain't that classic! The minute the law shows up the witnesses clam up." He planted both elbows on the bar and stared at each person in turn.

Nanette was the first to break the silence. "What in Sam Hill are you talking about, Chief? Have you gone plumb daft? Are you trying to tell us that there's something fishy about Bertha's death? As far as we knew the poor old soul keeled over from too much lard in her gravy. Are you saying that's not the case?"

An elderly waitress handed Pete a fresh mug of steaming coffee. He took a tentative sip and swirled it around in his mouth as if tasting fine wine.

"What exactly are you attempting to convey, Pete?" Laurence leaned back so that he was eye to eye with the police chief.

"Not a thing. Just that I know how you old fogies work. You don't have anything useful to occupy your time, so you go around making up stories. Creating drama."

"Chief, we are not playwrights, nor are we high school students. We were simply discussing the proposed new highway construction. It was you, sir, who turned the conversation into a dramatic production." Laurence looked amused.

Pete set his mug on the counter with a thump and stalked toward the exit. "Just remember, I am the law around here."

"Well what bee got into his bonnet?" Nanette asked as the door slammed.

"Methinks he doth protest too much." Laurence mumbled.

"Oh, stop talking like the King James Bible!" Nanette gave her old friend a playful shove and a thin stream of coffee splashed down the side of the cup.

"Not the Bible, dear lady. Our esteemed upholder of the law just reminded me of a line from *Hamlet*. Shakespeare," he added, "not the prophets."

"The way I see it," Nanette said, ignoring Laurence, "is that strange lawmen aside, we all have a lot of work to do. Do you really think we can find enough documentation to declare our library a historical building? Enough legal paperwork to keep it from being torn down?"

"I don't know," said Laurence, stepping away from the counter and pulling his hat from the rack. "But I bet you ladies won't rest until you find out."

"I'd say we should continue gathering up some numbers," said Marguerite. "Everybody respects numbers. Document how many people used the library this past year—how many checkouts, how much computer use—you know, statistics like that. If nothing else, we'll flummox them with figures. We'll daze them with data!"

Chapter 10

The last patron had left the building and Emma's stomach rumbled in anticipation of dinner at her dad's house. But that would be over an hour from now. It was still full daylight outside this time of the year and the sun cast a glow through the old windows of the library. A mockingbird in the walnut tree sang his repertoire with abandon. Emma allowed herself the luxury of listening to the concert for a few moments. Mockingbirds always reminded her of sitting with her mother on the porch of the old farmhouse.

I still can't believe old Miss Brubaker is dead, she thought as she placed the last book on the mystery shelves and wheeled the cart back toward the office. Her foot caught on the edge of a large cardboard box in the corner of the room. Easter decorations. Emma sighed. Easter had been over for two months and she still hadn't taken the box to the basement. Well, today would be the day, she decided. If Bertha Brubaker had the nerve to battle cobwebs and spiders, so did she.

The musty scent of old paper and mildew met her at the top of the steps. She flipped on the light switch and the dark room took on a ghostly glow. Emma carried the box gingerly down the steps and deposited it on the nearest shelf.

Turning to go, she caught a glimpse of a small leather book on top of a rusted file cabinet. Funny. She hadn't noticed that before.

The book was worn, but Emma could still make out the letters of the gold inscription at the bottom: Bertha Brubaker. She flipped through the pages. It was a planner. Bertha must have left it when she visited the vault. She felt a rush of anticipation at the discovery.

Back at her desk, she hesitated just a moment before she opened the cover of the planner.

An interior pocket held a small necklace in a zip-top bag and a letter from Dr. Nash's office. She looked inside an envelope addressed to William Brubaker. It was empty. The penholder loop was broken, and two disposable ink pens were clipped to the calendar's front page. Emma flipped the book open to May, and looked at Bertha's neat handwriting:

Tasks for May:
—Have Hiram get trunk from attic
—Call Billy
—Consult with Stewart—will
—(May 8) Dr. Nash, 9:00 a.m.—no breakfast!

A folded paper was tucked into the divider between May and June. Emma opened it. Written in strong, dark letters made with a permanent marker, it read, "And a man's foes shall be they of his own household." It was signed, "Hiram."

Her heart thumped in her ears. That sounded kind of threatening. Of course, Hiram was a strange man. Still, could this have anything to do with Miss Brubaker's death? She shivered. She should turn the planner over to the police, just in case. Even though it seemed obvious she'd died of heart failure or something like that. She grabbed her yellow spiral notebook and jotted down her thoughts beginning with Miss Brubaker's visit to the vault.

Satisfied with her ordering of events, she picked up the phone and dialed.

"Police department," said the voice on the other end of the line.

"Hello Pete, it's Emma." She tried to make her voice sound brisk and businesslike. "I thought you should know . . . I've just come across Miss Brubaker's planner here at the library. Do you think the sheriff's department will want it for their investigation, or should I just give it to Billy?"

"What investigation is that, Emma, my dear?" asked Pete, drawing out his words. "You know she was an old woman and she died at home of a heart attack. The autopsy is simply routine because she died alone. Are you suggesting something more sinister? Have you been

51

reading too many of those mysteries you have at the library?" He chuckled in amusement at his comment.

"No, Pete, I'm not suggesting anything," said Emma, her voice tinged with irritation. Pete was such a know-it-all. He always made her feel stupid. "I just thought the police might want it since she just died, you know?"

"Tell you what, sweetheart. I'll send Patrolman Dove over to pick it up in the next fifteen minutes. We'll see it gets into the right hands. You can wait until he arrives, can't you?"

"I guess so," said Emma. Leave it to Pete to delay her pleasant evening. "But I'm leaving in a few minutes. So please send Jason as soon as possible."

"Hot date, eh?"

"Well, that's none of your business, is it, Pete?"

"Woo-eee! Touchy, aren't we? Well, look for Dove in the next few minutes, sweetie."

"Fine, Pete." Emma rolled her eyes as she hung up the phone. What an incorrigible jerk! She clenched her jaw and made a sudden decision. She'd give Pete the planner all right. He obviously thought it was unimportant. But first, she'd make a copy of its pages and the papers inside, just in case. Emma's curiosity was piqued and she wanted to take a closer look for herself, maybe even go visit her friend, Sissy Lambert, Hiram's daughter. Was Hiram at the Brubaker place the night Bertha died? She headed for the copier. She had to hurry before Jason arrived.

Emma placed her copies inside a red file folder and tucked it into her carryall bag. She wrote a few more notes. She'd look through everything again when she got home later tonight.

A sharp rap at the library door made her jump, and she forced herself to relax so Jason Dove wouldn't notice her guilty behavior. Take deep breaths, she commanded herself. She stood for a moment until she had recovered sufficiently to open the door.

"Evening, Miss Kramer." Jason lifted his hat in greeting. "Shep here came along with me. I know you're closed, but he was hoping you'd let him use your fax machine. Hope you don't mind."

Emma forced a smile and gestured for the men to enter. "Okay. Give me your document and I'll fax it for you. And, Jason, here's Miss Brubaker's planner."

"Guess you're likely writin' up a storm about finding that planner." Shep gestured toward the open notebook on Emma's desk as he handed her two pages of handwritten notes and a slip of paper with a phone number.

The fax began to chug through the machine. Shep leaned on the wall and put a foot up behind him. "You always were quite the news reporter, puttin' together little stories around town."

Emma avoided meeting Shep's intense gaze and closed her notebook with a decisive flourish. She didn't owe Shep Crawford an explanation. It was a relief when the fax beeped.

"Here's your stuff, Shep. And that's twenty-five cents a page, so you owe me fifty cents.

Shep pulled the coins from his jeans pocket and placed them in Emma's hand. The brief contact made her cringe. She hoped he didn't notice.

The men departed and Emma straightened her desk. As she stepped out into the warm evening air, she felt a surge of guilt. But taking a look at the planner was the natural thing to do. Anyone would have done the same. Copying it might be a different story, though. She heaved her heavy bag to her shoulder and headed for the parking lot.

Chapter 11

On her way to the farm, Emma entertained herself by listing off the pleasing traits of Jake Preston. Polite. Handsome. Attentive parent. Great smile. It was nice to have someone new in town like him.

She didn't see the dented black pickup speeding up the narrow road until it was almost too late to get out of the way. She braked hard and slid into a shallow ditch. Dust and gravel sprayed the front of her small Toyota, coating the bright green finish with a dull gray. Who was that crazy driver? She turned and caught a glimpse of Shep Crawford at the wheel and his passenger ... Emma couldn't believe it! Serafina Wimsey! What an unlikely pair. What on earth could Serafina be doing with Shep? Did it have something to do with the fax she'd just sent? Emma sat with her hands gripping the wheel until her heart stopped racing. It looked as though she would need to get used to seeing Serafina around every bend in the road. It was only a matter of time until Serafina would sink her claws into that handsome new detective. Emma was sure of it.

When Emma pulled onto the familiar lane, the old Kramer Farm sign waved at her from its perch atop a rusty metal pole. That sign could sure do with a paint job, but so could the barn, and even the house, for that matter. As her car bumped over the grates, she could hear the Black Angus cattle lowing in the back field. At one time, her father kept over a hundred head. Today, he and her brother, Josh, were lucky if they could take care of twenty-five. The low price of beef and the high cost of grain was a familiar topic of conversation at the Kramer dinner table.

Her dad expected her to come to dinner once a week. Emma knew he was disappointed when she didn't show up, and she hadn't made it out here the last few weeks. Hopefully, the cookies she brought would help make up for it. She could picture the scene in her father's kitchen— Aunt Mia and Shirley, Josh's wife, taking the roast chicken, perfectly browned, out of the old oven, with the Parker House rolls sitting on the counter ready to bake at the last minute. When Emma was a little child she couldn't say "Maria." The best she could come up with was "Mia." The name stuck through the years. Emma couldn't remember a time in her life when Aunt Mia wasn't there for her.

Since her mother's death, her aunt had stayed close to the family, checking on her father daily, taking him home-cooked meals throughout the week. Just being there. The old two-story, white-washed farmhouse loomed straight ahead with the long gravel path leading right up to the front door. Wide-planked boards made up the wrap-around porch. That porch held a set of memories all its own. She and her mom used to sit on the wooden swing and wait for her dad to come in from the fields. She could almost taste the tart-sweet mixture of lemonade they sipped while they waited. The large, weathered barn sat to the left of the house. Emma saw her brother with his head bent over the tractor engine. He looked up in time to wave as she pulled the car to a stop, just next to a sprawling lilac bush. The heavy scent filled the air. Lilacs had been her mother's favorite flower. The old screen door gave a familiar creek as Emma opened it and went inside. She was home.

"Dad! Where are you? I come bearing gifts! Well, at least I made some cinnamon cookies for you!" She wandered through the kitchen into the living room. He was sitting in his favorite cushioned gliding rocker in the corner of the room with the newspaper spread over his lap, spilling onto the floor. He looked up and gave his daughter an apologetic grin. "Hey baby girl! So sorry about the mess." Charles Kramer stood up and gave Emma a hug. He was a medium-built man with graying hair and salt-and-pepper beard stubble covering his chin. "Ow, Dad! Your beard is scratchy! Are you growing it out already? I thought you waited until fall."

"Just too lazy to shave today. I'll clean myself up before long. What ya got there?"

"Cinnamon cookies."

"Oh my goodness! Haven't had those since your mother . . ."

"I know, Dad." Emma put her hand on his shoulder. "You know these won't be nearly as good as hers, but hey, you've gotta give me credit for trying!"

He bit into the soft cookie and his face took on an expression of mock rapture. "Ah," he said through a mouthful of crumbs, "pure ambrosia!"

"Come on, Dad, you know I'm not a quarter of the cook Mom was. She tried to teach me some of her secrets, but we both know I had better things to do!"

"Yeah, like follow Josh and me around all over the farm. Remember the day you almost fell into the sewage pond?"

"Now how fair is that? I bring you gourmet cookies and all you do is remind me of my childhood blunders!" She gave her dad a playful punch.

"Well, come on into the kitchen. I think your Aunt Mia and Shirley been puttin' together some kind of meal."

"Need some help, ladies?" Emma gave her sister-in-law a quick peck on the cheek and moved across the room to her Aunt Mia. Emma rested her cheek on the soft gray curls. For just a moment, she was able to relax and forget the stress that the past few days had brought. For an instant in time, she could imagine she was leaning against her own mother, feeling the warmth and comfort of unconditional love.

"It's so good to see you here my dear," Aunt Mia dried her hands on her apron. "Now why don't you give Shirley a hand?"

"Why, Emma Kramer! I thought you had moved out of the country! I don't think you've been over here since Easter!" Shirley's long brown hair was twisted into a braid and wrapped in a tight bun at the nape of her neck.

"Now you're making me sound like the prodigal daughter!" Emma grinned as she took the bowl of potatoes away from Shirley and began whipping them with the mixer.

"Hey, you give those back to me. We don't want to choke on potato lumps! Why don't you make yourself useful and go find that brother of yours? He's been messing with the tractor all afternoon. Tell him dinner is on the table and growing stone cold!"

56

The wind had shifted, and this time when Emma stepped into the open air, the pungent smell of cow manure mingled with the scent of lilacs. Ah, the joys of farm life!

Emma found her brother bent over the old John Deere, his handsome face screwed up in concentration. He didn't even know she was there. She had always admired that trait in her brother, that ability to stay focused on the task no matter what was going on around him.

"Hey Josh, can you spare a few seconds to eat dinner? Shirley says it's getting cold."

"Well, if it ain't my favorite librarian! I'd give you a hug, but I don't think engine grease would match your outfit."

"Uh, probably not. What's with the tractor?"

Josh took off his hat and passed a grimy hand over his sweaty face. "The better question is what's not with the tractor! I've been working on this piece of junk for two hours now, trying to get it started. Dad keeps telling me that the Deere never dies, but apparently I don't possess the particular power to bring her back to life."

"We had this tractor when I was little. It must be at least twenty-five years old by now!"

"Twenty-seven. I've replaced every movable part on the thing. I'm running out of options. Dad just doesn't want to face the facts. I really don't know how long we're going to be able to keep this farm going. We're maxed out on Farm Credit loans as it is."

"I hear what you're saying, Josh." Emma put a hand on her brother's arm. "There are a lot of things Dad can't seem to see clearly now that Mom is gone. But tell me, Josh, what in the world would he do without this farm?"

Both Emma and Josh turned as they heard Shirley calling from the back door, "Hey you two, soup's on, we're all waiting!" They walked back into the house in companionable silence.

When they were all seated at the round oak table, they held hands while their dad said the blessing. This was tradition as long as Emma could remember, giving thanks as a family.

"Emma, any more news about the library and that highway department proposal?" Charles Kramer tried to sound casual, but Emma noticed a tenseness in his voice.

Emma gave a deep sigh. "No Dad, I guess we'll all find out more at the public meeting. The ladies at the library are very concerned."

"The library isn't the only thing at stake, baby girl." Charles Kramer and Josh exchanged glances.

"Wait, you two aren't thinking this is a good thing, are you?" Emma's face grew hot.

"I just think we need to find out more information. Saw Tom Billings down at the co-op, and he seems to think the money they'll offer will be more than fair. Could be several farmers are taking this idea of selling out serious." Charles Kramer shifted in his chair.

"We have to look at our options, Sis! Farming is a hard life anymore. Getting harder every year." Josh's face flushed.

"I can't believe you two! How can you even think about not owning this farm anymore? It's been in our family for generations. It's hard enough to think about losing the library. I never thought for one minute that the farm would be a part of this disaster." A tear rolled down Emma's cheek and she wiped it away roughly.

"Baby girl, none of us want to give up the farm. Sometimes, life just doesn't turn out the way we expect."

Emma could see the hurt in her father's eyes. Why did things have to change? Why couldn't her dad and Josh keep the farm just like it was? Overcome by a longing for the safety and happiness of her childhood, Emma allowed the tears to flow down her cheeks, unchecked.

Chapter 12

Poison.

Justice Atkins sat on a tall stool next to the steel counter with the heels of his polished brown loafers hooked on the rail. An array of various test tubes, stainless steel instruments, and containers were neatly arranged on shelves above the counter, making it obvious to employees and visitors alike that the doctor prided himself on a well-kept laboratory.

Focused on the state lab report he had just printed off from his computer, Atkins was oblivious to the coworkers passing his door and poking their heads in to say farewell for the day. He flipped the pages of the report from the state lab back and forth, checking and rechecking the information. Yes, it was poison.

The report stated that the sample from Bertha Brubaker's body had indicated a lethal amount of belladonna at the time of her death. Deadly nightshade. That explained her flushed face when he'd arrived on the scene. He whistled softly through his teeth. So. It was either murder or suicide. He wondered if she'd received some bad news from her doctor and just decided to end her life. He'd seen it before.

Atkins stood up straight and exhaled loudly as he stretched his back, popping several vertebrae in the process. It had been a long day. It would be Detective Preston's job to find out what really happened. He looked on the report for Preston's number and punched it into his phone.

"Preston?" he said. "Glad you picked up. Atkins here, medical examiner. I have the report back from the state lab on the samples we sent in from Bertha Brubaker's body. I've just emailed you a copy. You're not going to like this, Preston. It's clear she died of poison. Belladonna.

So she either killed herself, or you've got a murder case on your hands." He paused. "Hope you didn't have any plans for tonight."

The rain fell in broken lines and hit the scattered puddles with the force of tiny pellets. Jake lifted the shade on the window beside his desk and watched as two robins pulled long earthworms from the soaked ground. They didn't seem to mind the rain, or even notice that water drops were dancing off their feathers. He turned from the window and stared once more at the folder on his desk. The true story behind Miss Bertha Brubaker's death: poison. Highly unlikely it was suicide. Maybe, but she wasn't the type.

The report from the lab said belladonna, dried and possibly mixed with a liquid substance. Tea.

Jake didn't want to speculate. Not now. Not until there were more pieces to this puzzle. But at least he knew what he had on his hands. Death by unnatural causes. Suicide or murder. Not old age, not a sudden malfunction of the heart.

Jake grabbed his phone and headed down the hallway. He punched in a number and held the phone to his ear while he pulled his keys out of the front pocket of his trousers. He'd almost reached his car when a voice came on the line.

"Lab."

"Yeah, this is Jake Preston. I need a team back out at the Brubaker house right away. Just learned the cause of death was poison. Maybe ingested in a cup of tea. Anyway, you'll need to take the kitchen apart and see if you find any traces of belladonna." Jake nodded as he slipped into the driver's seat. "Yep, that's right. Belladonna."

Allowing himself to exceed the speed limit, he arrived at the Brubaker mansion in just 15 minutes. He took the porch steps in two large strides. Good. The door was still locked and the yellow caution tape was still in place. Jake sat down on the top step with a sigh. He'd wait right here for the officer he'd called. Until the forensics team had finished gathering evidence, he'd assign a guard. He hoped he hadn't botched the investigation by leaving the place unguarded before now.

It was time to call Billy and let him know what the lab report showed. He'd be livid about having to stay out of the house but Mr. Brubaker needed a reality check. Because if Bertha Brubaker had been murdered, Billy was suspect number one.

Chapter 13

Oh to have an administrative assistant, Emma thought as she checked the packing list against the box of books that had just come in. But alas, there was barely enough money to pay her salary, much less support another staff member. There was just too much for one person to do. She arrived 45 minutes early today to try to catch up on some book orders. It was only Tuesday, but she was wishing for Friday already.

But it was a good job for her, given the course of her life in the last few years. The unexpected arrival of Serafina brought back so many memories. Up until her last year of college, Emma's future still held exciting possibilities. She and Eric had mapped out an amazing trip across Europe after graduation. They'd trek the ancient rocks of the Western Uplands, navigate the Thames, and hike the Alps. Then they'd get married and move to the coast where he could continue his studies in marine biology. She'd work in a big-city library. But now, thanks to Serafina, Eric was dead.

It wasn't as though Serafina had set out to be malicious. Emma doubted if her ex-friend sat still long enough be calculating or even intentionally hurtful. Serafina just *was*. She was as elemental as the earth, as volatile as fire—the fire that had started the whole mess.

Of course it had been Eric's choice to go to the party. Or had it? Back in high school, rumor had it that Serafina was learning how to make magical potions like the old mountain folk. Maybe Serafina had charmed Eric with an elixir.

No, thought Emma ruefully, the only spell Serafina had cast was that of her irresistible self. Emma couldn't blame Eric, really. After all, what good would blame do? Eric was gone. A victim of being in the wrong place at the wrong time. A guest at a party that served too much alcohol, provided too many drugs, and was alight with too many unattended candles.

Just a week after Eric died in the fire, her dad had called to tell her that her mother's "indigestion" was terminal cancer. They had no idea she was that sick. Her emotions in turmoil, Emma was unable to focus on completing her coursework. The dean granted her permission to finish the final term's work during the summer, at home with her dying mother. Emma didn't graduate with her class. It was the lowest point of her life.

Only once did Emma speak to Serafina before she left the university. She wanted Serafina to admit her responsibility for Eric's death. Of course, in true Serafina style, Serafina denied charming her way into Eric's life and encouraging him to go to the party.

Emma still had dreams about the fire and Eric. And Serafina. Emma was still in shock that Serafina had returned to Custer's Mill.

It was three years since her mother's death and her dad was finally starting to get back on his feet. A year ago, Emma landed the job at the library and in January she'd moved into a brand new townhouse. Her life was getting a fresh start, right here in good old Custer's Mill.

Emma walked to the copier to print off some order forms. When she opened the lid, she gasped. In her haste last night, she'd left Hiram's letter on the platen. She was becoming careless. Lucky for her somebody else hadn't found it first. She'd give it to Jake. Or Pete. Soon.

She had just slipped the letter into her red folder when he library door creaked open. The door was unlocked, but she didn't expect her volunteers to arrive for another 15 minutes. It was Pete Anderson, clutching a bouquet of late spring flowers and looking sheepish, like a young schoolboy.

"Hello, Pete. Coming to do some botany research?"

"Very funny, Emma. Actually, these are for you. Do you have a vase or something you can put them in?"

Emma sat down on the desk chair and gave Pete a puzzled look. Pete was bringing her flowers? Whatever for?

"C'mon, Emma. Take them. This is my way of apologizing for being such a jerk on the phone yesterday. I don't know what comes over me sometimes. But you and me, well, we've known each other a long, time, and it's important to appreciate those old friendships. So, here you go. I'm sorry."

"Wow. I don't know what to say," said Emma. She didn't want to tell Pete she'd never considered him a friend—old or otherwise.

"How 'bout 'Thanks, Pete'?" The tinge of sarcasm was more like it. Sarcastic Pete she could understand.

"Um, thanks, Pete," repeated Emma, reaching for the flowers. "I'll get a vase from the back room. I think there's one that these beauties will fit in. Yeah, thanks."

Emma retrieved a vase from the storage room and returned to find Pete leaning with one hand on a stack of magazines. Had he seen the folder? She glanced at the desk. No, it was just peeking out of her denim bag, unremarkable. She thought of Hiram's note. She should give it to Pete.

"Aw, you look pretty when you blush." Pete smiled his familiar lopsided grin. "Don't worry, I'm not trying to hit on you. I'm sorry about the way I spoke to you when you called about that planner. I was out of line."

"Thanks, Pete. Really, this is so thoughtful."

"I know you don't think much of me, Emma. But I've always thought you were one of the smartest girls in town and I'd like to count you as a friend. So, peace?"

"Sure, Pete. Peace."

He flashed her a peace sign and walked back toward the door.

She arranged the flowers in the vase and put it on her desk. Very pretty, she thought. And very confusing.

Maybe she'd misjudged Pete after all.

Chapter 14

Jacob Craun motioned directions as the feed truck driver backed slowly into the dock. Today was going to be a busy day at the Custer's Mill Hardware. Feed delivery, quarterly inventory, and a pressure cooker check for the canning folks in the area. Pulling a large red bandana from his back pocket, he wiped the sweat that was already forming on his brow. Unseasonably hot for this time of year.

The stock boys had just begun to unload large bags of corn when Jacob heard loud voices coming from inside the store. He gave the driver a quick nod and walked into the store and stared in surprise. Billy Brubaker and Hiram Steinbacher were engaged in what appeared to be a shouting match.

"So why did you kill my Aunt Bertha? Didn't she give you enough money? Even you wouldn't be dumb enough to think she'd leave you anything in her will!" Billy was standing with his face only inches away from the Brubaker estate's peculiar gardener.

Hiram stood, tight-lipped, against a display of onion sets. The gardener's face was a dark shade of red and the white bristles of his beard stood out in contrast.

"What's the matter? Can't you answer a simple question? I want to know what Aunt Bertha ever did to you?"

"Never avenge yourselves, but leave it to the wrath of God, for it is written, 'Vengeance is mine, I will repay, says the Lord.'" Hiram took a step backward into a row of rakes. The first in line toppled over, causing the others to crash to the floor.

Jacob Craun stepped between the two men. "Now look what you've done! Do you two think I don't have anything to do but clean up after you? Look. I don't care if you two beat the crap out of each other. Just get out of my store!"

By that time, a small crowd had gathered. Jacob glared at the group. "Show's over, folks! Gentlemen, make your purchases and move along."

Hiram quietly began to hang the rakes on hooks as Billy continued to glare at him.

Nanette Steele, pressure cooker in arms, glared at Billy. "What's gotten into you, man? First, we don't even know for sure how Bertha died—"

Billy interrupted. "Yes we do! Atkins called me this morning. Poison. Belladonna poison. And look who grows herbs in his spare time!" He glowered at Hiram again.

Nanette let the pressure cooker fall to the counter. "What? Poison? What do you mean? Did somebody kill Bertha?"

Billy stared. "Maybe I said too much."

"You, my friend," said Nanette, closing in on Billy's face, "did not say enough! What do you mean?" she repeated. "Are you telling me that Bertha was murdered?"

"No, not exactly murdered. She could have done herself in. You know. Could have taken the poison herself."

"Are you completely crazy, man? Bertha Brubaker was a religious woman who loved life. There is no way she would have deliberately taken her own life!"

"I don't think she did." Billy looked at Hiram who was continuing to hang up the rakes in silence. "All he would have to do is slip poison into her tea or even into her spaghetti sauce. Shoot, he could have put it into any one of her herb jars."

"Good grief, Billy. Get yourself together." Nanette picked up the pressure cooker again. "What does Hiram have to gain? No motive, no murder."

Billy grunted.

"Besides," continued Nanette, "Speaking of motive, take a look in the mirror. If anybody profits from Bertha's death, it's you!"

Billy's face turned red. "How dare you, you interfering—"

"Not rocket science Billy. You stand to inherit a tidy sum from Miss Bertha."

66

Before Billy could respond, Hiram stepped over to join the group. Looking directly at Billy, he cleared his throat. "We both know what you've done." He turned and left the store without a backward glance.

Nanette left the hardware store in a flurry. She had to tell the others about the fate of their old friend.

Emma's townhouse was first on her way home. She hammered on the doorknocker. Emma appeared, coffee mug in hand, eyebrows raised in surprise.

"Nanette! Come on in. I was just about ready to leave for work." She looked at Nanette with concern. The woman's face was flushed and she'd skipped her usual greeting.

"I won't stay long, Emma, but I just had to let you know in person. Bertha died from poison! I just saw Billy at the hardware store and he'd heard from the coroner this morning. Poison! Billy said that she could have done herself in, but I don't believe it for a minute, and he obviously doesn't think so either. He accused Hiram of murdering her!" Nanette paused to catch her breath.

Emma stared at her friend, stunned. "Poison? Really? That's horrible! What are the police doing? Are they opening a murder investigation? I need to find out from Jake. Or Pete."

"I'm sure that Jake will do a good job. But to think there might be a murderer in our little town . . ." Nanette shuddered. "Well, I'm off, but had to give you the news right away. I'm stopping by Jane's next, then Marguerite's. After all, Bertha was one of our library's greatest supporters. This is a shock."

Emma waved goodbye to Nanette. Slowly she pulled her spiral notebook from her denim bag. News of Bertha's poisoning made Hiram's note of warning even more sinister. She really must give that note to Jake as soon as possible. But first she'd do a little investigating on her own. Just in case Jake or Pete might miss something important.

Chapter 15

"Thanks for driving us over here, Emma." Jane tightened her scarf. "It's eerie coming here now, knowing Bertha died of poison. And this whole idea of picking out her burial clothes feels strange. I don't think I've even been in her bedroom before."

"But it would have been even weirder for Billy to go through her things," Nanette said. "And I'd hate to think what Reba Dove would have picked out! I'm glad that Jake Preston gave us permission to come back to the house. It's the least we can do for our poor old friend. About time she finally gets a proper burial."

Nanette dug into her canvas tote and pulled out a plastic bag. "Here. I even remembered to bring along a bag to put the clothes in."

"A plastic grocery bag?" Marguerite shuddered. "I'm sure we can find a suitcase in Bertha's room!"

Nanette huffed. "Suit yourself, Miss Priss. Plastic grocery bags have served me well for many a year. Don't see why they're not good enough to use now."

"Well, I guess we can't sit in this buggy all day. Let's get this job done!" Jane climbed out of the car and motioned for the others to follow.

They stopped in front of the mansion. Yellow police tape stretched across the porch.

The officer on duty motioned them up the steps and held the tape so they could slip underneath. "Detective Preston said you could have 15 minutes, ladies. And don't touch a thing except the clothes you're taking."

He held the door open, and the friends stepped into the still, dim hallway.

"Probably my imagination, but doesn't it feel like this house knows Bertha's gone? I mean, it looks kinda gloomy. Like the life just went right out of it."

"Can we hit the lights?" asked Marguerite, just as Emma found the switch and flooded the hall with brightness.

"Oh, my!" Marguerite gasped. "What happened in the parlor?"

The ladies peered into the room where the quilt from over the fireplace lay crumpled on the floor, pictures hung at varying angles, and the secretary drawers gaped half open, papers spilling on to the floor.

"Good grief! Wonder if the police did this? Or was it like this when they came back?"

"I don't know," said Jane. "But this is not how it looked the day she died. Bertha would have a fit!"

"Emma, dear, maybe we should check with Billy to see if there is a simple explanation for this. Could you call him, while we go up and find what we need for the funeral home?" Marguerite's voice shook. "Billy may want to come over himself and talk with the officer."

"All right, ladies, you go on upstairs, and I'll see if I can track down Billy at his office."

Emma pulled out her cell phone and dialed Billy's office.

"Town Manager, Billy Brubaker."

"Billy, this is Emma. Emma Kramer. I'm here at Bertha's house. Well, your house now. I'm with the ladies, getting Bertha's clothes for Johnson's. I'm calling to find out if you know why the parlor is in such disarray. Drawers are open and the quilt is on the floor. I don't think the police did this. I wondered if…well, if someone got in here before the police came back over." Emma took a breath. She heard the ladies upstairs moving around Bertha's bedroom.

"The police were there for a couple of hours last night. I wouldn't worry about it too much. It's not your concern, Emma. I'd like you and the ladies to just get the clothes and leave."

Emma felt herself flush. Billy's tone was condescending.

"Okay, but I think you might want to come later and see for yourself. It is your family's house, after all. Goodbye, Billy."

Emma felt a stab of guilt for giving into sarcasm. She knew Billy couldn't deal with Bertha's clothes for the funeral home, and she felt sorry for his loss. But she couldn't understand why he seemed so unconcerned about the house. She tucked her phone away. Determined at least not to leave the antique quilt in a heap on the floor, she gently folded it and draped it over the back of the sofa.

The ladies were still upstairs. Emma decided to seize the opportunity do a little investigating of her own. She checked to make sure the officer wasn't looking in the window. Then pulling out her notebook, she scribbled a few notes as she scrutinized the room.

Surely Jake or Pete wouldn't have allowed a crime scene to be contaminated like this. She moved around, righting the pictures that were hanging askew and peeking behind them. She wondered if someone had searched for a wall safe.

Her sleuthing skills now on high alert, Emma stopped in front of the secretary. She leafed through the disordered papers. Most appeared to be Bertha's household receipts and routine bank statements. Nothing of special interest. She knew the ladies would scold her for being nosy. When she heard them at the top of the stairs, she quickly walked over to the doorway.

"Jane, I don't think Bertha will care if we put her in taffeta or polyester at this point." Nanette's voice echoed in the spacious stairway. Jane carried Bertha's funeral ensemble in a clothes bag. Nanette had a pair of shoes in her hands, and Marguerite followed with a small overnight bag. They looked like they were on their way to a senior citizen's sleepover.

"Is Billy coming to check things out, dear?" asked Jane.

"Not right now, so we need to lock up the house."

She didn't want to tell them that Billy was unconcerned about their discovery. Letting the others file out the door, Emma glanced back over her shoulder. What could someone have been looking for?

Chapter 16

Jake watched Emma across the small round table at the Bard's Nest bookshop. He was glad she'd agreed to meet him here. He really needed some background on Custer's Mill. Over the past few days, as he was putting a plan of action together to investigate Bertha Brubaker's death, he realized what a disadvantage being new in town was for him. He hoped Emma didn't think this was a date. He was way too rusty to start dating again.

"Jake, you're a million miles away." Emma took a sip of the tall cream soda in front of her. "I guess you have a lot on your mind with Bertha's death, right?"

"Sorry, my mind was wandering. Yes, once Atkins's report came back, we knew we were dealing with a poisoning," said Jake.

"So, it's official. Bertha was poisoned. How? What was it?" Emma rummaged in her purse for her notebook.

Jake frowned as he watched Emma write several lines in her notebook. "Whoa, Emma, this is now a questionable death investigation, and I shouldn't say any more."

"What type of poison was it, Jake? Something easily accessible? How do you think the poison was administered? You certainly can't think Bertha poisoned herself!"

Jake stared at Emma. "I thought *I* was the investigator!" He reached over and closed Emma's notebook. "We have to look at all possibilities and suicide is one possibility. The other is that someone planned to murder Miss Brubaker. Can you think of anyone who would want to harm her?"

"But Jake," Emma protested, "I suspected all along that Bertha's death was suspicious. She was in perfect health and had everything to live for. I think it's obvious it wasn't suicide."

"Oh really?" Jake frowned. "I think we need to stick to the original purpose for our meeting. Remember, you were going to fill me in about Custer's Mill."

"All right, I can take a hint." Emma slid her notebook back into her purse. "There are two places in town where the people of Custer's Mill gather to share news and gossip—the Spare Change Diner and here at the Bard's Nest. I'm surprised Laurence George lets anyone drink so near his precious books!"

Jake looked around the cozy bookstore. "Hopefully we're too far away to ruin too many volumes!"

Emma took a sip of her drink. "He gets some sort of joy in reminding me that he makes a lot more money than I do with his 'for profit' book venture. I really wish the government wouldn't feel so inclined to publish our salaries in the local newspaper every year."

"Yeah, mine is in there too. One of the joys of working for the state."

"So why did you move here, Jake? I should think you would make a lot more money in Northern Virginia."

"More money but the cost of living is ridiculous. I was paying $1,800 a month for a small, two-bedroom apartment in Winchester."

"So that's why you moved?" Emma knew she was prodding, but couldn't stop herself.

Jake hesitated, and then said, "No, it wasn't just the money. Kate's relatives are from this area, you know."

Emma raised an eyebrow. "Really? I thought I knew everybody in Custer's Mill."

"This was a bit before your time, Emma." Jake smiled. "Kate's great-grandmother was Ruth Porter."

Emma looked up in astonishment. "Really? But Ruth was . . ."

"I know. African American. Now you're trying to figure out Kate's blond hair, aren't you?" Jake smiled and continued. "It seems that each of the Porter women had a fondness for light-haired men."

"So you're bringing Kate back to her roots, so to speak."

"Yes, that's one reason." Jake paused.

"Oh, there's more?" Emma propped her elbow on the table, resting her chin in her hand.

"Yes. But I'm not sure I should go into that now."

"Well you have to now. You have my curiosity fully engaged!" Emma smiled.

Jake cleared his throat. "Well, I'll give you the abbreviated version. Kate's grandmother, Kath Porter, was killed in a fire when my wife, Mirabelle, was just a toddler."

Emma nodded. "I vaguely remember my parents talking about that a long time ago. A firecracker incident?"

Jake passed a hand over his face and sighed. "That's what the newspaper articles said. I'm not quite so sure. Many of the so-called facts don't add up. Now, I'm not saying that my only reason for moving here is to open up that investigation again. But being in the area does offer more opportunity to add to my knowledge about the incident."

Emma straightened suddenly and almost knocked over her drink. Catching it in one hand, Jake smiled. "What's this? A sudden revelation?"

"Yes! My great-uncle Albert! He's lived here for ages, and he's a superb local historian." Emma's words tumbled out as she became more animated. "After all, he taught history at the University of Virginia for years! I'll bet he remembers the fire. I'll bet he knew the Porters too. We have to go talk to him!"

"Do you think he'd be willing to talk to me? After all, I'm practically a stranger."

"Uncle Albert knows no strangers!" Emma assured him. "Are you free Saturday? We could drop Kate off at the Saturday Morning Club at church. She'd love that! Besides, I was planning to visit him to talk to him about the library building and how we can get it registered as a historic landmark. And he can certainly tell you more about the history of Custer's Mill than I can.

"If anyone can help us both, it's Uncle Albert."

"Why sure, I'd love to go with you," said Jake, pleased and surprised. "So what's this Saturday Morning Club like, anyway? I'm a rather protective father, you know."

Emma smiled. "Protective is good. The pastor and his wife came up with the idea and are on hand almost every Saturday. Gives the kids something constructive and fun to do—mostly crafts and games. It's very popular with the under-ten crowd."

"Okay, I'm in! What time shall I pick you up?"

"This is my idea, so I'll pick you and Kate up at nine thirty."

They sat in silence for a few minutes and then Jake said, "Shall we call it a night then?"

Emma yawned. "Yeah. Six o'clock comes early."

"Got big plans tomorrow? It's your day off, isn't it?"

"I'm planning to visit an old school friend. Haven't seen her for a while. We have some catching up to do."

As they left the diner, Jake noticed the old green van before he saw the grizzled figure sitting on a nearby bench under the streetlight.

"Good evening." Jake nodded his head in greeting.

"Vanity! All is vanity and vexation of the spirit!" mumbled the ragged man.

Jake raised an eyebrow. "Is something troubling you, sir?"

Hiram looked up, but his greasy baseball cap was pulled low on his brow and neither Jake nor Emma could see his eyes.

"It's a world of sin we're living in. Wrongs need to be set right." Hiram rose suddenly from the bench and headed toward his van.

"And who was that?" Jake asked as soon as Hiram was out of earshot. "I saw him out at the Brubaker place."

"Oh, he's weird but harmless. In fact, he's the father of Sissy, the girl I'm going to visit tomorrow. His name is Hiram. Hiram Steinbacher. He was Miss Brubaker's gardener."

"Well there's an unlikely pair!"

"Indeed."

Chapter 17

Where do lost dreams go? Sissy Lambert folded a faded dish towel and placed it in the laundry basket. Do they circulate back into the universe and land on somebody else? She sighed. With her husband's unsteady construction job, they couldn't plan on moving out of the double-wide any time soon. The dream of the Cape Cod and the white picket fence would have to wait. Again.

She wanted the house to look as good as it could though. Emma Kramer had never been to her place before, and she wanted her friend's first impression of her little place to be a good one. Such a lovely day! Late spring sunshine seemed to show the house in a favorable light.

And then a cloud floated over her mind. She hadn't seen her daddy for several days now, not since Miss Brubaker died. Miss Brubaker had always been nice to her father, not like the townspeople who thought Hiram was eccentric and walked wide circles around him. But how could she blame them? Her father lived in that old green van, refusing to stay with her and her family. His brief time with them had been a disaster. Hiram complained about Harold and the kids having the TV on all the time.

Sissy and her father had argued for days, until Hiram finally declared he could no longer live with such evil and filth. The devil's tool, he called it! She was so deep in thought that it took a moment for her to register the fact that the old Chevy van was pulling into its usual spot on the gravel parking pad—almost as if her memories had conjured it out of the air. The van gave a sputter and a jerk as Hiram turned off the ignition.

"Godless fool!" Hiram was cursing someone, but Sissy just couldn't make out who it was.

"Daddy, what in the world?" Deserting her laundry, Sissy moved across the lawn toward her father.

Hiram was oblivious as he opened the side door of the van. His wild raging continued. "The wise woman builds her house, but the foolish pulls it down . . . *pulls it down*!" Hiram emphasized these last words by punching into the air with his fists.

Sissy was worried. This rant seemed more than his usual mutterings.

"What is pulled down? What's happened?"

"He that is perverse in his ways . . ." Hiram stood at the side of the van shaking his head. Sissy pulled gently on the sleeve of his shirt, trying to bring him back.

"Sissy, girl!" Hiram's face softened as he realized his daughter was at his side. She looked into her father's eyes and saw a deep sadness.

"Daddy, what is going on?" She stroked her father's sleeve as she would a child's she was trying to console.

"It's that godless Billy Brubaker. He told me to get off his land— his land! And how long has it been *his* land, Sissy? Why Miss Bertha's body was scarcely even cold when he ran me off! Wicked, godless man."

"Well, I guess it is his land now, but who does he think is going to take care of that place if you don't? Billy Brubaker's never done a lick of hard work in his life."

"Sissy, you know Miss Bertha trusted me with her gardens. For twenty-five years, I've pruned her roses, trimmed the bushes . . . done everything that needed to be done. And now Billy Brubaker thinks he can come strolling in and take it over? And that's not the worst of it! After all those years I helped that woman while he sat on his backside, Billy has the gall to accuse me of murdering her!" Hiram was shaking now, his anger bubbling close to the surface. "The house of the wicked will be overthrown." Hiram once again shook his fist into the air.

"Well, enough of this. Do you want to come in for some iced tea? I just made a pitcher with a few sprigs of spearmint fresh from the garden."

"I've got something to do here in the van." As Hiram pulled open the side door, Sissy looked at his sparse living quarters. Her eyes scanned the only two pieces of furniture: an old brown, plastic recliner and a small wooden table. Shelves, lining the left inside wall, held various

76

items such as gardening tools, lanterns, old engine parts, and a row of large brown boxes. A small refrigerator, hooked up to the car lighter, served as his only way of storing food. But her father didn't need much to sustain him. He usually ate at the diner.

Sissy watched as Hiram shuffled through the boxes, finally taking down the one he was looking for.

"I'm just going into the house to get you that iced tea! Be back in a minute." Sissy waited to see if he would answer her, but Hiram ignored her. He placed the box on the table and took off its lid, pulling out the contents piece by piece. Sissy shook her head and hurried toward the back porch of her trailer.

A few minutes later, she returned, balancing a tall glass of mint tea and a carafe. As she approached the side of the van, she could see her father sitting at the table staring at something that looked like a picture.

Hiram's voice rose once again in a threatening tirade. "Woe to the wicked! Disaster is upon you! You will be paid back for what your hands have done."

"Daddy, here is your tea." She stuck her arm inside the van and gave him the glass, placing the carafe on the floor next to the table. She tried once again to change Hiram's train of thought. "Guess who is stopping by? Did you hear me? Guess who called me and is stopping by this morning?"

Hiram, realizing Sissy had been watching him, put the picture facedown on the table and slid it under a pile of papers from the box. "I'm listening to you girl. Now, who is it that's coming over?"

"Emma. My old friend Emma Kramer." Relieved that she had her father's attention, Sissy gave a weak smile and continued. "Remember how close Emma, Serafina, and I were growing up? Three peas in a pod, that's what Momma called us. We went everywhere together—school, camp, dances. Yep, we were inseparable. That is, until they went off to college." A slight sadness edged into Sissy's voice.

Hiram slammed the papers back in the box, abruptly getting to his feet. "I don't want to see nobody. I've got to go!"

Sissy watched in despair as her father put the box back on the shelf and stepped out of the van. "Daddy . . . I know Emma would like to see you. Can't you just stay for a few more minutes?"

"No! I told you girl, I don't want to see nobody, especially not some busybody sticking her nose in somebody else's business, always writin' in that notebook of hers!" Hiram bellowed, as he closed the side door with a bang and moved around the front of the van to get into the driver's seat. Starting up the engine, he backed into the street without looking.

"Stop, Daddy!" Sissy ran down the driveway, calling out a warning as Hiram nearly hit Emma's small car.

For a brief minute, Hiram's steely eyes bore deep into Emma's. Then the van moved off down the road, the old muffler rumbling.

"Emma, I'm so sorry! Daddy just isn't himself lately, not since Miss Brubaker's death. I was sure he would stay to see you, though." The two friends hugged.

"It's okay! I don't think he saw me driving up the street. Let's go inside. We've got lots to catch up on."

"You still like raspberry iced tea, Emma?" Sissy carried a small tray to the kitchen table and placed it in front of Emma.

"Ah yes! Remember when Bessie Crawford invited us to tea that summer? She told us she was giving us Earl Grey and it tasted more like dried grass with fake sugar."

Sissy giggled. "Remember what Serafina told her? She accused the old woman of trying to kill us! Those were the days." Sissy's eyes took on a faraway expression.

Emma tried not to let her eyes wander, but it was difficult not to notice the faded plaid wallpaper in the living room and the worn floral sofa that sagged on one side. The cream-colored crocheted afghan, neatly folded over the back of the sofa, managed to calm down the clashing patterns and bring a homey feel to the room. Emma remembered Sissy's mom had tried to teach the girls to crochet when they were ten.

"What was that?" Emma's mind quickly snapped back to their conversation when she heard Sissy mention Serafina.

"I was just asking if you had talked to Serafina," said Sissy. "How long has it been—five years?"

Emma shifted in the chair. "Serafina is back, you know. I just saw her at the library. I don't know where she's been these last few years, or what she's been doing. You know Serafina. Always a mystery."

"Emma, that's wonderful! Let's plan a get-together soon, for old time's sake."

Choosing to ignore Sissy's suggestion, Emma pulled out a folded piece of paper from a small spiral notebook. "Sissy, I'm glad we could catch up on old times, but I also came today to have you look at something." Emma pushed the note across the table.

Sissy carefully unfolded the paper and let her eyes wander over the uneven script. Her face drooped with disappointment. "So I guess this is really why you came. This was written by my father. Where did you get it?"

"I found it with some things Bertha Brubaker left at the library. The note was in her planner, so I assume Bertha read it." Emma paused.

"Well, it looks like one of Daddy's verses. He likes to quote the Bible, you know." Sissy folded the note and gave it back to Emma. "Like I said before, he's been awful upset by Miss Brubaker's death."

"But, it seems like a threat of some kind. Or maybe a warning?"

"What are you getting at?" Sissy began to shake her left foot, rattling the ice in the glasses.

"I'm just trying to find out what happened to Bertha. Think about what the verse says, Sissy. *And a man's foes shall be they of his own household.* Could your father have been trying to warn Bertha Brubaker? Could he have suspected her life was in danger?"

Sissy sat silently for a minute, her lips pressed together. "I know that my daddy was beholden to Miss Brubaker. She was the only one to give him a job. She was the only person in town who saw something good in him. I know that note looks bad, but why would he want to hurt her? But you're right: it does sound like a warning, like he was trying to tell her to watch out. My daddy worried about Billy—and others—takin' advantage of Miss Bertha. He said so many times."

"Do you know where you father was when Miss Bertha died? Was his van in your driveway? If you knew where he was, you could give him an alibi."

Sissy carefully shredded a small paper napkin and arranged the pieces on the vinyl tablecloth. When she looked up at Emma, her eyes were troubled.

"I don't know where he was, Emma. Sometimes he parks his van in town and some nights he stays on the Brubaker estate. But he wasn't here. His van wasn't parked out front."

Emma looked sharply at her friend. "You're sure?"

Sissy nodded.

"I'm really sorry, Sissy. I have no choice but to give this note to the police. I thought maybe you'd be able to verify where your dad was for sure." Emma folded the paper and tucked it back in her notebook. She looked at her friend in sympathy.

Sissy's eyes began to fill. "Why, Emma? Why do you have to do that? It's just a note with an old man's rantings. It doesn't mean anything."

"It might, Sissy. Besides, I've held it longer than I should have." Emma moved toward the door. "I should have given it to Jake before now and he'll probably be mad I've kept it so long. It could be a lead to who killed Bertha Brubaker."

Chapter 18

The day was hot and bright. Emma rolled the windows down as she waited in her car while Jake dropped Kate at the Saturday Morning Club. She was nervous. But it was time to 'fess up. Now, before they headed over to Uncle Albert's house.

As Jake climbed back into the car, Emma took a deep breath and held out Hiram's letter. "I know I should have given this to you sooner, and I apologize. It was left behind at the library when Jason Dove came over to pick up Miss Brubaker's planner. It . . . um . . . it fell out and I didn't notice it until later."

Jake read the note and looked at Emma through narrowed eyes. "This could be important evidence in the Brubaker case, Emma. You should have turned it in sooner."

"I know. I said I was sorry, Jake." Emma glanced at her lap. "I hope you're not mad at me."

Jake folded the note and put it in his pocket. "I'll let it go, Emma. But please don't do anything like this again."

"I won't," Emma promised. She was glad the air was cleared. Now she looked forward to introducing Jake to Uncle Albert. The outing wasn't ruined as she feared it might be.

Emma pulled the car into a short gravel drive beside the small gray-stone cottage. A wall running along the shady side yard was covered in ivy and brightened by vigorous purple blooms of interwoven clematis. Old flower beds, neglected and overgrown with tall weeds, lined the perimeter of the yard and house, but Emma remembered a time when they were neatly kept with old-fashioned peonies, fluffy white hydrangeas, and giant hostas. She could still see the plants through the weeds, patiently waiting for a willing gardener to pull back the curtains.

Emma pressed the yellowed doorbell and gave Jake a sideways glance. The chime echoed softly inside the house, and after a brief wait, the wrinkled face of retired Dr. Albert Nelson appeared in the window at the top of the door, his glasses perched on his considerable nose and his expression a mixture of irritation and curiosity.

"Come in, my dear girl!" Professor Nelson opened the door and made a courtly gesture inviting the two young people to enter. "And who might this be?"

"Uncle Albert," said Emma, "This is Jake. Jake Preston. He's the new county detective."

"Pleased to meet you, Detective," said Professor Nelson. The two men shook hands. "And to what do I owe the honor of your visit?" he asked. "But ... before you explain, let's sit where we can talk comfortably. Please," he nodded toward a green flowered chair. "I'll put the pot on for some tea. You do like tea?" He looked sternly at Jake, his glasses slipping even further down his nose.

"Yes, sir," answered Jake. "Tea would be wonderful."

"Good," said the professor, with a firm nod of his head. He picked up a gnarled walking stick leaning against the wall, and moved with measured steps into the kitchen.

Jake raised his eyebrows and exchanged a quick look of amusement with Emma. Emma smiled and gave a small shrug as she followed the professor into the kitchen.

Jake moved several *History Today* magazines from the chair to the floor and sat down. The small room smelled of old wood and paper. Books filled the built-in china cabinet, and two large wooden bookshelves overflowed with double rows of books and stacks of magazines squeezed into every possible space. Stacks of papers surrounded the ancient computer sitting on the antique walnut desk in the corner, and a large gray cat slept curled on the padded desk chair, undisturbed by the arrival of guests.

Emma and the professor returned shortly with a tray of delicate china cups and a steaming pot of fragrant tea. With no available space on the crowded coffee table, Emma placed the tray on the floor and crouched down as she poured each of them a cup. Emma and Dr.

Nelson settled themselves on the sofa, and Emma sighed with contentment as she looked around the room, remembering magical childhood visits she had made to this home.

"Well, Uncle Albert," said Emma, "let me explain why we've barged in on you today. In fact, we have a couple of things we'd like to talk to you about." She smiled at Jake. "We're here to ask you about some local history."

The professor set his cup down and smiled. "Now that's one area I can help you with. What do you need to know?"

Jake looked at Emma. "Why don't we start with the library building?"

Emma nodded. "Uncle Albert, have you, by any chance, heard about the state's plans for a new highway in Custer's Mill?"

The professor shook his head. "They've been talking about that for as long as I can remember."

"Well, now, the talk's more serious. In fact, Billy Brubaker, came in the library the other day with a guy from the highway department. And what's worse, they're planning to tear down the library building!"

"Tear it down?" said Professor Nelson with alarm. "No, I didn't know. That's a travesty. That's a crime! It must not happen." He put his teacup down on a pile of *Smithsonian* magazines and stood up, pacing back and forth across the small room with his cane in his hand. "My dear, my dear," he muttered. "It must not happen."

"Uncle Albert," Emma said softly. "It's going to be all right. Tell us what you know about the building. We'll do everything we can to stop this plan."

Dr. Nelson resumed his seat on the sofa and adjusted his glasses.

"That building was built by the Brubaker family when they moved here from the coast in 1832. They first used it to conduct business and as living quarters while their large manor house was under construction. When they moved into the big house, they converted part of the original building into housing for several of their household slaves. Family records I've seen suggest only the most trusted slaves were allowed to live above the business, although Charles Brubaker didn't take any chances, and he closed off the downstairs to them. They used a separate entrance at the back of the building. Elsie Porter's great-grandparents were among the first married slaves chosen to live there.

The Porters stayed on as servants after the Civil War—Elsie was old William Brubaker's housekeeper for years."

Professor Nelson glanced out the window as if lost in reverie. For a long moment, Emma thought he might have fallen asleep. But he shook his head abruptly and continued.

"During the Civil War, the family used the entire building for storing food and even preparing meals for soldiers, including Union soldiers who came through toward the end of the war. It was a field hospital for a short stint. It's a miracle the entire Brubaker place wasn't burned when Sheridan came through. It must have caught the eye of some Union general—maybe he thought he'd buy it from the Brubakers or something."

Professor Nelson rose and began to pace again as he continued.

"There are indications from various Civil War–era letters and documents that the building was used as a stop on the Underground Railroad. Near the separate entrance the slaves used to access their quarters, there is supposed to be an entrance to the building's cellar, where a false wall was built to hide slaves running from their masters." Professor Nelson flicked an imaginary speck of dust from his sleeve.

"So there might be some historic significance to the building? Maybe underground tunnels?" Emma's voice rose in excitement.

"Maybe. But I've looked for that wall, and never did discover it. Some of these places had tunnels, but no one has discovered one in this building so far. There were also often special markings on or around buildings that signified safe haven for runaway slaves. Since the Railroad was so secretive, the documentation is sketchy at best. But I want that building left intact. Not only is it valuable in its own right as a very historic building—you know it became the town hall after the Brubakers donated the building and adjoining property to the town—but I want to find out if it has even more significance as a stop on the Underground Railroad. Tearing it down would be a travesty . . . a travesty."

Dr. Nelson shook his head as he continued to pace and look at the floor. Emma rose and put her hand on his back. He leaned heavily on his cane and looked absently at her face, his mind far away.

"Uncle Albert," she said soothingly, "please don't fret. We're going to fight this. But if you can find any documents or information about the building and its significance, would you let me know right away? That would be a tremendous help to us."

"I most certainly will, my dear," said Dr. Nelson. "You can depend on that. If this is the last thing I do, it may well be the most important work of my life." His voice shook with emotion.

"We should go now," said Jake, rising from the chair.

"But we haven't asked—"

"That's okay for now," Jake smiled. "The professor has enough to think about at the moment. Besides, it gives us an excuse to come back. And aren't you going to the Brubaker funeral?"

Emma nodded. "I do need to get back soon."

"Goodbye my dears," muttered the professor. He gave Emma a quick hug and shook Jake's hand. He returned to his desk, too agitated to see them to the door.

Chapter 19

Lula Parker's mezzo-soprano voice filled the high ceilings of First Methodist Church.

"*Rock of Ages, cleft for me.*"

Emma shifted in her seat, half expecting that gentle bell-like pitch to break or to at least quiver with age or anxiety. But the tone remained true to the end.

"*Let me hide myself in thee.*"

"Not half bad," Nanette murmured. "Pretty clear voice for a woman of middlin' years."

"Whatever does that phrase mean? 'Middlin' years'?" Marguerite's whisper was less audible than Nanette's, but it was still loud enough for several people in the row ahead to half turn in their seats.

"Middle age. It means middle age, for heaven's sake! Just because you lived half your life in the city shouldn't make you forget how we talk in the country."

Marguerite folded her hands in her lap and looked straight ahead, clearly ignoring Nanette's jibe.

Bertha Louise Brubaker was laid out in a fine state. The staff at Johnson's Funeral Home had taken extra care with the makeup and clothes the library Friends had chosen. The stalwart threesome would not budge until they were assured their friend would look "as natural as a dead woman could look," as Nanette had phrased it.

The pews were packed with a variety of townsfolk, all dressed in their Sunday best. Everyone was coming to pay his or her last respects to the matriarch of Custer's Mill.

A whiff of patchouli wafted up the aisle. Serafina had arrived. She slid into the pew behind Emma and the library ladies. "Wow! This place is packed! And most of the people are old. You know, I sometimes think old people enjoy funerals."

Nanette glared. "Show some respect, girl. You won't be young forever."

Serafina smiled. "I have a few years yet. Ooooh! Look who just walked in!" Tossing her long ginger hair back from her face, Serafina turned her turquoise eyes to the back door as Jake Preston made his way up the aisle, holding his daughter's hand.

"Hey! Here's a spot!" Serafina turned a dazzling smile toward Jake and patted the pew beside her. Jake grinned. "Thanks!"

Emma turned toward the newcomers. Kate still held on to her father's hand even though the pair had sat down. The little girl looked solemn and wary. Why would Jake bring a child to a funeral? To be honest, though, she knew her aggravation had little to do with a young person's exposure to death and everything to do with the titian-haired goddess sitting behind her with the detective. It felt like college all over again. What kind of spell did this woman have?

The Reverend Stephen Winston made his way to the podium as Lula sat down. He surveyed the crowd and smiled. "Yes, I do believe Miss Bertha would be pleased at this marvelous turnout. Happy that so many of you are willing to share in the celebration of her long, productive life."

Emma gave up trying to focus on the minister's words. The scent of patchouli was too strong behind her. Instead, she looked at the crowd of people in front of her. Hoyt Miller's son, John, had returned to Custer's Mill for the funeral. Half a dozen years as a big city criminal lawyer had given the former high school homecoming king the shrewd eyes and jaded expression of someone who had spent too much time with the dark side of human nature. He was still good looking though. So was his wife, who despite being the mother of three, could have been a supermodel. Emma wondered if they were happy. Things looked good on the surface.

"As we pay our last respects to this pillar of our community," the reverend was saying as Emma pulled her attention back to the service, "is

87

there anyone who would like to speak in Miss Brubaker's honor? Perhaps a story or an anecdote to share with her friends and family?"

Nanette was the first to stand. "Well, I was never one to go along with Bertha's fancy ways and china tea cups." A titter broke out among the audience. China cups went the way of the rubbish bin when Nanette had tea at Bertha's. "She was a generous woman. A woman who had a lot but also gave a lot to this community. She was always funding projects at the library and always helping out here at the church. I, for one, will miss her." Nanette blew her nose and sat down.

Reba Dove spoke next. "I cleaned for Miss Bertha for nigh onto forty years. Never once was she late in paying me, and every Christmas there was something extra in the envelope."

There was a lull in the conversation, and everyone looked at Billy. Finally, he rose to his feet and cleared his throat. "My Aunt Bertha was a good soul. She went to a lot of trouble to see that I was looked after when my parents died. I reckon I owe her a lot." He sat down and put his face into his hands.

"Well that was a poor excuse for a eulogy," Nanette grumbled.

Reverend Winston rose to give the final prayer. Then, a thin, reedy voice spoke up from the back. "Vengeance is mine, I will repay, saith the Lord. Touch not mine anointed one." Hiram Steinbacher stood, twisting his cap in his hands.

Nanette started to speak but Marguerite hushed her. "Let the man finish," she hissed.

"Thirty years I have toiled and earned my bread with the sweat of my brow. Thirty years I have watched the hand of justice move slowly. Now is the dawning of the truth. This day the truth is upon us. Take heed that you be not led astray."

Silence filled the sanctuary. It was a long moment before the reverend recited the prayer.

Chapter 20

Jake Preston pulled out a cool metal chair and sat down among the other citizens of Custer's Mill. The place was packed. This highway project was certainly close to the heart of the townsfolk. Jake smiled as he noticed the library Friends sitting with Emma on the front row. Although he hadn't been in town long, he already knew the library ladies well enough to realize that he would not want to oppose them in a controversy like the highway placement. There was an empty row of chairs directly behind the library group. Jake wondered if it was empty on purpose. He abandoned his seat at the back and moved toward the vacant seats.

"Hello ladies."

"Why if it isn't the handsome lawman!" Nanette grinned. "I hope you've chosen the side of the just and right in this little matter."

"Of course. I just got to know this little library. I sure don't want it torn down!"

"Good man," said Nanette with satisfaction.

At the end of the row, Jake glanced at Serafina who was tapping her foot restlessly against the wall. She was hard to miss. That ginger hair and those eyes . . . He was drawn back into the present with a loud whisper from Emma Kramer.

"Mutt and Jeff."

"What?" Jane Allman, directly beside Emma also heard the comment and followed Emma's gaze to the door where Pete and Billy had just entered.

"Pete is so tall and muscular and Billy is short and squat. They just remind me of that old comic strip my mom used to collect. Two men

89

with completely opposite looks and personalities. Josh and I used to crack up when we read those old magazines."

"Nothing funny about that one." Jane nodded toward Pete. "Looks like he had a tall glass of prune juice right before he left the office!"

"And poor Billy! He just lost his great aunt and now he has to deal with this town mess," said Emma.

"Great turnout," whispered Marguerite as she turned to look at the growing crowd of people filling the metal chairs lined up in the chamber room.

"Wonder how many people Billy-boy has brainwashed this past week?" Nanette said loudly. Several people twisted in their chairs to look at Nanette.

"Shhh! You want to get us kicked out of here?" Jane jabbed her friend sharply in the ribs.

"Ouch! You beast! Did you just file those elbows?"

"Ladies," hissed Marguerite, "act your ages! Now, be quiet, both of you. The meeting is about to start."

Hoyt Miller, chairman of the town council, struck the gavel to begin the meeting. "All right, let's all settle down and take our seats. I now call this meeting to order. Reba, will you please read the minutes of the last meeting?"

Jake's mind wandered as Reba's voice droned on. He glanced over at Pete Anderson who was leaning against the wall. He wondered why the police chief didn't just sit down. Maybe he wanted to show off the 9mm pistol that bulged on his hip. Showing off was probably the only action he got in this town. Except for Bertha's death, Jake corrected himself. Or possible murder, to be more accurate. He still couldn't wrap his mind around the idea that somebody might have gotten rid of the town matriarch. Belladonna poisoning, of all things. In his years of detective work, he'd never run across a death by belladonna poisoning. He turned his attention back to the meeting in front of him.

"We all know the purpose of this meeting. There's only one item on the agenda tonight: the new road that is coming right through our little town." Hoyt cleared his throat.

The room buzzed with voices. Nanette leaned back and put her mouth to Jake'. "Well, this ought to be good. You know some people already have their minds made up."

Marguerite put her hand up in protest. "Don't be so negative, Nanette; let's give the process a chance. After all, this is a public meeting, and we are here to become more informed about this road."

"Ladies." Hoyt scowled. "We're here to discuss business. Mr. Jarrod Harmon is here from the Department of Transportation. He's going to give us an overview of the proposed highway and how it will affect our town. I give the floor to Mr. Harmon."

Jarrod looked as though he had just stepped out of a glossy men's magazine. His dark hair was slicked back and his gray, pinstriped suit appeared to be tailor-made, pressed and creased at all the right angles.

Nanette gave a low whistle.

He flashed a perfect set of gleaming white teeth to the crowd and walked over to stand beside a laptop and projector. It was rare, in the small town of Custer's Mill, that the council meetings included such a professional presentation.

"Good evening, ladies and gentlemen. Thank you for taking time from your busy schedules to join us for this informational meeting. I hope you will find some food for thought in my presentation." He clicked the mouse and a large map of Virginia appeared. A long, wavy yellow line streaked across the map through Custer's Mill.

"As you can see, the proposed Highway S will run from the port of Norfolk across the state of Virginia, connecting with major interstate roads, giving coastal access to trading destinations in the southern United States." He paused to let this sink in, and then continued. "This road will cross some of the most rugged terrain in the eastern United States, improving access to national forests and historic landmarks."

Jarrod looked out over the audience. A few faint grumblings and muffled comments flitted around the room. "Again, I want to assure each and every member of this community that my team is watching out for the residents of Custer's Mill, as well as the state of Virginia. Why, we have mapped out a route that protects the environment as well as the historic sites in our beautiful state." He continued to flip through the slides showing scenes of mountain streams and abundant wildlife in their natural habitats.

"We know what our state looks like," said a gruff voice from the back. Hiram, Emma suspected. "Just get on with the show."

Jarrod adjusted his tie and smiled. "You are perfectly correct, sir." He nodded in Hiram's direction. "Ladies and gentleman, I have not come to show you what you already know about this beautiful state of ours, but rather, how this road will bring commerce and tourism to our state and raise the economic development right here in Custer's Mill."

With that comment the room droned with excited voices.

"And what about our land sir, as well as the rich history tied to this area?" Professor Nelson swept his hand across the area as if the "rich history" were contained in the room. "Many of the residents live on farms that have been in their families for generations. The Brubakers settled this area before the Civil War. They built their wealth on trade and did not need a superhighway to do so." The room exploded in cheers and clapping.

Hoyt banged the gavel on the granite tabletop and tried to bring order back to the meeting. "Please, everyone, take your seats. You're out of order, Professor Nelson. I can see that we have many people who feel strongly about this subject. I propose we delay further comments until the next meeting."

Jarrod spoke quickly to quiet the audience. "We are ready to generously compensate those people who own farms on land needed for the proposed new road. To our way of thinking it is a win-win situation." He stopped as the room totally erupted in pandemonium. People began to rise to their feet.

Hoyt stood up, his face red with anger. "Order! Order!" Emma leaned toward Nanette, "I've never heard that man raise his voice in all of the years I've known him." The loud command, however, from the usually easygoing Hoyt had the desired effect.

As the citizens of Custer's Mill took their seats, the noise in the room began to subside. Hoyt spoke in a normal tone. "At the next meeting, citizens will be allowed to speak for or against the new road. If you wish to be on the agenda, come up front and give Reba your name. We will see you back here next Monday. Hopefully, you'll have learned some public-speaking etiquette by then."

Jake stood and glanced around the room. Already there was a line forming at the front, folks who wanted to add their name to the list to speak at the next meeting. Professor Nelson and Hiram Steinbacher led the charge.

Chapter 21

The town meeting lasted longer than Emma had hoped. Still, it was productive. Both sides had a lot to think about. She slung her blue denim bag over her shoulder and headed to her car, keys in hand. The distant mountains still glowed with a faint outline of light. Emma loved nights like this. Tonight she planned to simply relax. It had been a long day.

As soon as she pulled into her driveway, she saw it—glaring cold and sharp. Her front window was shattered; nothing remained but a gaping hole surrounded by jagged shards. Broken glass glittered on the holly bushes below, dimly lit by the streetlight.

Was it a stray baseball? A rock thrown up by a mower? She mentally reviewed her homeowner's insurance policy. They'd cover the damage at least. She walked to the stoop to see if anyone had left a note of explanation on her door. That's when she froze. The front door appeared to be slightly ajar. Emma's body trembled as she slowly backed out onto the street and climbed back into her car. Was someone inside her house? With shaking hands, she dialed 911.

She gripped the steering wheel, hands white and lips set in a severe line, waiting. In minutes, Jason Dove pulled up in a Custer's Mill police car. And right behind him was Jake, in a county vehicle with flashing lights. The lights were bad enough, but at least neither car was running sirens.

Relief flowed through Emma as she stepped out of the car. She resisted the strong urge to run and throw herself into Jake's arms.

"Well, Jake, we meet again," she said, attempting to appear lighthearted. "I'm probably overreacting. Maybe a kid threw a wild pitch with a baseball. But the door looked slightly open, so . . ."

"Come on, let's take a look." Jake motioned for Jason to lead the way. Emma's heart pounded as he pushed open the door and stepped inside.

The room was in complete disarray. Broken china littered the floor next to the walnut buffet. Papers and magazines were strewn across the floor. The closet door stood open and boxes and their contents lay scattered around the room. A large rock rested against the foot of the rocking chair. Shards of window glass littered the floor. Her cat, Molasses, meowed plaintively from the corner of the room. Emma picked him up to comfort herself as much as the cat. She swallowed hard to force back tears. That was her mother's china. She loved it.

Jason looked at Jake, eyebrows raised. "I'll take a look around, sir," he said.

Jake nodded. "Okay, but take it slow and be careful," he said. "You're the responding officer here, Dove. I'm just backup."

Jake pulled on a thin pair of latex gloves he had stashed in his pocket and picked up the rock, hefting it gently in his hand like a softball.

"There's something taped to it," he said. "It's a note."

He carefully peeled off the paper, unfolded it and read, his face serious.

"Let me see," Emma stepped over broken glass to peer over his shoulder.

"You're in over your head, sister. You're being watched." The words were scrawled in large block letters.

Emma's stomach lurched and a cold chill ran down her spine. "It's a threat!" she said, her breath coming in short gasps. "Someone is threatening me! Jake, do you think this has to do with the planner? Or the note I found?"

Jake frowned and squeezed her elbow. "I don't know, Emma. But we'll find out who did this. Right now, you need to find another place to stay."

Emma looked around the room. She wouldn't cry. She would focus. Focus on the practical details. Where to go? If her dad learned his daughter's house had been broken in to, it would be too much for him to handle in his present state of mind. Her brother would rant and rave about finding out who did this, and only upset her further.

"I'll call my Aunt Mia," Emma said aloud. "I'm sure she won't mind putting me up for a few days until we get this sorted out."

"I'll wait right here while you go pack, then I'll follow you to her house."

"Okay. I'll take Molasses with me." She buried her face in the cat's fur and tried to recover her composure. "Aunt Mia loves cats."

Emma called Mia as she went upstairs to pack. As expected, Mia insisted that Emma stay at her old Victorian house on Myrtle Street, a place Emma loved as a child. She felt safe there.

"I have plenty of room," Mia was saying. "If I don't see you within fifteen minutes, I'm coming to get you myself."

"I'll be there," said Emma.

Emma carried her suitcase and the cat carrier downstairs, dread and terror increasing with each step.

Chapter 22

Emma lingered in her car a few minutes, taking in the sight of the familiar old Victorian house. White lace curtains moved slightly in the front turret windows. It was comforting to know Aunt Mia waited inside.

Jake's cruiser came to a stop behind her.

Emma jumped out and popped up the handle of her roller bag. With her denim bag over one shoulder and cat carrier in hand; she gave Jake a wave and a thank you. Before he could get his seat belt off, she was on the front steps.

He watched her until she was safely inside.

Mia opened the door and Emma was immediately folded into a tight, protective hug. "Emma, dear, I've been worried since you called." A feeling of warmth and love flooded over Emma. She began to cry.

"Dear, dear. You're safe now. Let's sit down. I've made us some tea." Emma followed Mia past the huge center staircase that dominated the hallway. It brought back memories of herself as a child, sliding down the banister of the plush carpeted steps and holding on to the round knob of the newel post to swing herself to the floor.

She followed Mia to the plump rose-colored sofa, and let Molasses out of the carrier. He scampered under the walnut sideboard..

Emma wiped her eyes, then sank into the softness of the sofa. She could smell freshly baked bread and some sort of ginger potpourri. She leaned back into the overstuffed mounds of pillows. Mia tossed her a handmade shawl embroidered with pink rosebuds. "Here, get cozy while I check on the cookies.

Mia returned with a tray of steaming hot tea and a plate of cookies.

Emma sniffed. "Just when I felt like I was getting my life in order here in Custer's Mill after the mess at college and Mom's death, everything has turned upside down. Miss Brubaker has died, the future of the library is in jeopardy, Serafina is back in town, and somebody threatened me."

"Threatened you! Good heavens, girl! Tell me again what happened." Her aunt sat down on the edge of the sofa.

"Well, when I drove up to my house this evening, I could see a big hole in the front window. I knew better than to go inside, so I called 911." Emma paused as tears spilled from her eyes. "The house was trashed. And whoever it was broke some of Mom's china."

"Jason Dove and Jake Preston both answered my 911 call. They searched my house, but didn't find anyone. But they did find a rock that was thrown through the front window. A note was attached. It said, 'You're in over your head, sister. You're being watched.'"

Emma stopped again for a moment, composing her thoughts. "Jake waited while I called you. He insisted on following me here."

"Absolutely, you should not stay in that house!" Mia said. "But why would someone threaten you?"

"Well ... I think it has to do with Bertha Brubaker's death. I found something of Miss Bertha's in the library—her planner. There were several items in the planner, including a strange note from Hiram Steinbacher."

"This sounds like something the police should have, Emma. You did give it to them, I hope?"

"Yes, Aunt Mia, they have it. After I copied everything, I gave the planner to Pete and Hiram's note to Jake."

"Emma, this could be very serious. Why in the world did you make copies? And now you're being threatened! I hope this Jake will look into it."

"He will, but I was doing a little investigating of my own. I wasn't sure the police would really follow up on the things I found in the planner."

"Emma, I love you, but you've always been just a bit on the nosey side. Now your curiosity has gotten you into trouble." Mia narrowed her eyes. "Do you still keep a journal?"

"It's right here in my bag. Along with my copies of the planner."

"Emma, have you ever thought maybe someone is looking for your notes?"

"It's possible I guess." Emma shrugged. "But I haven't written anything that implicates anyone. The only person who ever wanted to see my journals was Serafina, back in high school."

"About Serafina," said Mia. "I hadn't wanted to mention her, but since you brought it up, why is she back in Custer's Mill after all these years?"

"She says she is going to open a tea and herb shop in the old flea market building. She's back in town and acting like she hasn't been away five years."

Mia put a hand on Emma's shoulder. "You have a choice, you know. You can decide whether you want to be friends with Serafina this time around."

"I just feel like I have too many things to think about right now." Emma's eyes began to fill again.

"You always have me . . . and the rest of your family. You're not alone."

Emma smiled weakly and continued, "It's more than this threat. All the talk about the new road, tearing down the library, and the highway department buying up farmland. I'm afraid Josh and Dad are going to sell the farm. You heard them at dinner. I don't want them to sell. It's all that's left of Mom."

Mia stroked Emma's hair. "I know you love that old farm. We all do. There are so many good memories there. But Emma, you must face the facts. The farm is losing money, and your father is not getting any younger."

Emma's head ached. She sat up and took a deep breath. "I think I'd just like to lie down for a while. Maybe a little rest will help me think more clearly—about everything."

"That's a good idea. Nothing has to be decided right now. You're safe here. You can stay as long as you like. Take the cookies up with you, dear. I'll call you in about an hour for supper."

Emma gave her a hug, then climbed the stairs, carefully balancing the cookies and her luggage. Her favorite room had always been the one at the top of the stairs to the right. It was a bright, sunny, yellow room with a turreted window and a yellow and pink floral bedspread on the white four-poster bed. Emma dropped her bag on the floor and put the plate on the nightstand. She went to the window seat, pulling her knees up so she could rest her head on them. As a child, she loved to sit here and look out over the backyards and gardens of the houses, dreaming of what her future would hold. Right now, she longed to be that child again.

Chapter 23

"Come in, come in." Billy Brubaker's voice was jovial, but his smile was tight.

Jake stepped inside the spacious two-story home. He knew Brubaker was nervous and trying to mask it by talking too much. He was pretty tired himself. He hadn't slept well after dropping Emma off at her aunt's last night.

Jake took note of a large white trash can in the kitchen straight ahead. The domed cover was sitting on the kitchen floor and the can was piled high with empty microwave dinner boxes. Stacks of dirty dishes were visible on the granite countertop. In the hallway and living room, Billy had hung a few framed pieces of stock art on the walls, but they were dwarfed by the soaring cathedral ceilings. The furnishings were sparse and monotone, and it was obvious that Billy lived here alone, without benefit of an interior decorator. He wondered if Brubaker was trying to give the impression of the well-to-do bachelor—from the street, at least. Inside, it just looked like a big, empty house that lacked warmth and companionship.

Jake felt sorry for Billy. He was suddenly grateful for his own simple house. Without Kate, he'd be living this same kind of empty bachelor existence. Though he could use some help decorating his house and making it cozier. Mirabelle had been good at that.

"Please, come in and sit down. Welcome. Welcome to my humble abode." Billy gestured widely with his arm and Jake walked through an arched opening into a spacious living room. It was a new home, with a great view of the mountains through the French doors that opened onto an empty deck at the far end of the room. Newspapers and documents were strewn across a glass-topped coffee table. Two overweight cats, one tabby and one yellow, blinked at Jake from their spaces on a brown sofa that was covered with liberal amounts of cat fur. The yellow cat meowed at Jake as if in greeting, then returned to grooming itself.

"That's okay. I'll stand, Mr. Brubaker," said Jake. "This won't take long. I just need to ask you a few questions about your aunt." He flipped open the cover of his notebook.

"Call me Billy, please. We're not formal around here."

"Okay, then, Billy. Were you on good terms with your aunt?" Jake gave Billy a direct look.

"Why of course! We didn't have any other close family left—we just had each other. And now, it's just me." Billy looked down and studied his hands. "I'm going to miss her. She made the best teacakes."

"As far as you know, are you the sole heir of her estate?" asked Jake.

"Yes, of course. Paul Stewart, her lawyer, will be reading her will in the next few days. But she always talked like I would inherit her place," he added in a defensive tone. "It's the family place. The ancestral home."

"Right," said Jake. "Did your aunt have any enemies in town? Anyone who would want to do her harm?"

"Well, she had some strong opinions, but that's not enough to make someone want to kill her, I don't think," Billy said.

Jake nodded as he made notes. "Do you know how your aunt felt about her gardener, Hiram Steinbacher? I understand you've asked him to stay off the property."

"Word gets around in this town, doesn't it? Well, he's a weirdo, Detective. I always wished my aunt would have sent him packing years ago."

"Why's that?"

"She took him on after he got out of jail when he was about twenty years old or so. He went to jail for setting a fire." Billy cleared his throat. "He was a big drinker back then. Rabble-rouser. Bad seed, you know? Spent about a year in the slammer, and she decided to take him on as a goodwill project and help him get out on parole. Then he got married and settled down. But he's just weird—he's gone all religious now, since his wife died back in the late eighties. I can't stand being around him."

"Anything else you think I should know about your aunt?"

"No, sir, not a thing. She was quite a lady. Quite a lady, indeed."

"Okay, Mr. Brubaker . . . Billy. Thanks for your time. I may have further questions for you later."

"Righto, Detective. You know where to find me." The yellow cat meowed again and stepped gingerly across the disarray on the coffee table. Billy picked up the cat and began stroking its head. "Yessir, I'll be around if you need me."

He walked with Jake to the front door and waved good-bye, balancing the big cat on one shoulder. The man and the cat had certain similarities in hair color and girth.

Jake sat in his car and made some final notes. Was Billy as fond of his aunt as he declared himself to be? If so, why was he so nervous? He was definitely hiding something.

One thing was certain. As the heir apparent, Billy stood to gain a great deal of wealth by his aunt's death.

Chapter 24

Serafina struggled against the wind that was trying to simultaneously blow her off the sidewalk and shred her umbrella as she tried to open the door. The antique brass key always stuck in the lock. Today the wood was swollen in the humidity.

She was determined to make the Serendipity Herb Shop the talk of Custer's Mill when she had the grand opening next month. She knew most of the citizens instinctively distrusted the name; even if they weren't sure what *serendipity* meant, it had a New Age sound to it. Reba had gone as far as to start a petition to deny the special use permit, managing to solicit exactly three signatures before she finally gave up.

Several town residents brave enough to enter its doors had stopped by earlier in the week. They were pleased to discover they could buy herbs and spices at reasonable rates—her products were much less expensive than the discolored dried stuff that filled the tin boxes at the big supermarket in Mill City. She hoped she'd soon get enough business to keep the shop open during weekdays. For now, though, she'd have to keep her part-time job as a waitress at the Spare Change Diner.

The sweet smell of cinnamon and nutmeg greeted her as the heavy door finally swung open. Serafina looked around with pleasure. The shop looked like a life-sized jewelry box. Rows of cobalt, ruby, emerald, and amber bottles gleamed on the rough-hewn shelves. Scarlet and turquoise silk curtains framed the high arched windows, and the wide wooden floor planks were covered in hand-woven rugs of yellow, blue, and green.

Serafina was just unpacking a box of essential oils when the bell above the door chimed. She looked up to see the long-limbed form of Shep Crawford ducking to come through the small doorway.

"Good morning, Shep!" Serafina was determined to someday elicit a smile from this taciturn man. Glancing at his rain-soaked jacket and dripping hat, she decided that this was probably not the day to do it.

Shep took off his baseball cap and smoothed his thinning hair. "Mornin' Miss Sera."

"Sit down and dry off a bit!" Serafina pointed to several mismatched chairs in the front of the room.

He folded his long legs into a small chair by the window and looked out at the rain washing down the guttering and gushing into the street.

"How's your grandmother?" Serafina pulled a chair from behind the counter and sat near Shep. She could smell the wet wool of his jacket and an indefinable musty scent that seemed to be part of the man himself.

"Not good." He twisted his hat in his hands and looked down at the floor. "She sent me to pick up some basil plants. Said you told her she could have some. And she sent you this recipe. Said you'd asked her about it." He pulled a wrinkled sheet of paper from his pocket.

"Please thank her for me—so nice of her to remember I wanted to try it out. And I saved her a couple of baby plants. They're in the cold frame out back. Wait here and I'll get them." She eyed the yellow raincoat hanging on the hook behind the counter and opted not to take the time to put it on. The rain pelted her as she lifted the glass panel from the small raised bed and carefully lifted four fledgling basil plants. Lord knows she owed old Bessie Crawford more than a few sprouts. The woman had taught her everything she knew about herbs, natural healing, and homeopathy. Bessie had also showed her a few other recipes and infusions—mixtures of a darker kind.

"Here, let me wrap these in plastic for you. You don't want to get dirt all over your truck."

They both glanced out the window to where the old '78 Chevy LUV pickup waited patiently in the rain. "Not much you can do to hurt that one," Shep said.

105

Serafina giggled. "I'll bet it could tell some stories, though. Stories about all of the babes you drove around town back in the day."

Shep blushed, and Serafina realized too late that the man's sense of humor in no way resembled her own.

"Want some herbal tea to ward off this damp? I'm gonna make a cup for myself."

"Nah, I gotta get back. Might talk the old woman into going to the doctor today. She's ailing."

"I'm sorry, Shep. What do you think is wrong?"

"Old age," he said simply. "She's goin' on ninety-six years old. She's wore out."

"So, Shep," said Serafina. "I just thought of something that might ease her a bit. Let me get it for you."

Serafina hummed as she filled a small envelope with a dried substance and sealed it shut. She handed it to Shep and walked with him to the door.

"Tell her to mix it with the wildflower honey. It'll lift her spirits. And try to stay dry." Serafina returned to the counter.

So many plants, so little time.

Chapter 25

By the time Emma arrived at the next public hearing, the council meeting room was almost full. Jake was sitting in the back row, alone. She was about to slide in next to him when Jane waved at her from the front of the room. "Emma! Come and sit with us good people. Scoot over, Nanette! You don't have to take up two chairs."

"Oh be quiet, Jane." Nanette kicked the seat in front of her.

"Nan, you can't let them get to you! Have a little bit of faith in our good professor! He'll set things straight today."

Nanette didn't answer, but slid over and gave Emma a space to sit.

Hoyt called the meeting to order.

"Before we begin, let's pause for a moment of silence in memory of our town matriarch, Bertha Brubaker, God rest her soul."

The crowd fell silent and men removed their caps.

After an appropriate pause, Hoyt resumed the meeting. "Last week, when Mr. Harmon made his presentation about the new road, many of you wanted to a have chance to present your views about this project. That's what this meeting is for—a chance for you to have your say." Hoyt paused. "Now just because this is an open forum doesn't mean you can disregard all rules of public speaking. You each have five minutes to say your piece. Be polite and to the point."

The early evening sun was shining through the southwest windows. Emma shielded her eyes with her hand so she could see the front of the room. She was anxious to hear what her Uncle Albert had to say. If anybody could charm an audience, her uncle could.

She looked over at the professor. He looked spiffy this evening, decked out in his best tweed suit. She craned her neck to see where Hiram was sitting, but couldn't find him. She was eager to hear what was on his mind. That man could deliver an evening's worth of entertainment in a five-minute speech!

She turned her attention back to the podium. Billy was about to speak.

The Custer's Mill town manager looked over the crowd as if searching for a friendly face. He cleared his throat several times before he spoke.

"You all know that the town of Custer's Mill was built on my family's land more than 150 years ago. The Brubakers owned over five hundred acres. Now my great-great-great-grandfather—" Billy paused and pretended to count on his fingers. "I think I've said enough greats! Anyway, this man had a lot of business sense and he could see into the future."

Nanette turned to Emma and whispered loudly, "Bet the man would have refused to have kids if he could have seen what an idiot this one has turned out to be! Bertha would be furious."

Marguerite glared at her, and Nanette settled back down in her chair.

Billy continued, "That's why he shared this chunk of land we now call Custer's Mill. Now I am nowhere near as smart or as business savvy as my ancestors. But I'd like to think I inherited a little of that DNA." Billy waited, but there were no nods or murmurs of affirmation. "Anyway, I can see the road having a positive impact on the economy and growth of our little town. I think we should strongly consider moving with the times and giving our support to this highway.

"You all know how hard it is to keep your farms going these days. Why I know for a fact, several of you have been thinking of selling out. This here is an opportunity falling right into our laps. Don't think this kind of windfall will come your way again. The highway department is ready to pay good money for your land, and help put Custer's Mill on the map."

Billy gave a mock bow and sat down to a smattering of applause.

The next few speakers owned small farms. They talked about the difficulties of keeping their heads above water with prices of feed going through the roof. Even though they were quick to acknowledge the fact that their lands had been in their families for generations, this money was too good to pass up. It would help them to start over and provide for their families without the headaches of keeping a dying farm alive.

Emma was getting worried. She glanced over at her father and brother, who were nodding in agreement. She had expected some farmers to be tempted by the deal the highway department was dangling. But she didn't think the road project would get this much support. Emma hoped her uncle could make a strong case for saving the library. Maybe put some perspective on the heritage that would be destroyed in Custer's Mill if this road went through.

"Sellouts!" Nanette made no attempt to lower her voice. Several people turned to scowl at her outburst.

"I sure hope Albert can pull some magic out of that beret of his." Marguerite looked worried as she watched Professor Nelson make his way to the front of the room.

Despite differences of opinion, most everyone in the room showed their respect for the professor, and the murmuring died down as he stood behind the podium.

"Citizens of Custer's Mill," he began, "you have known me a long time. Many of us went to school together and a lot of us have been friends for over sixty years. I have watched you take over your family farms. I've seen your pride in the land and your determination to keep the farms going. We have all worked together to make Custer's Mill a great little town and a safe place to live."

He paused. "What do you think is going to happen when this superhighway runs by our front doorsteps? I tell you Custer's Mill will never be the same." Several people nodded their approval. Hardware store owner, Jacob Craun, scowled and whispered to his neighbor.

Professor Nelson placed both hands on the podium and leaned closer to the audience. "Something Billy said really hit home. His ancestors gave this land so Custer's Mill could be established. Maybe some of you have forgotten that the year was 1853, eight years before the Civil War started. One of the first buildings constructed in the new town was the original Brubaker building that is now our library. There are records establishing the date of this building and documents that support its importance during the Civil War."

The professor leaned back and scanned the room. "I feel it is our duty to protect the heritage of Custer's Mill and the place it has in Virginia's history. In fact, I feel so strongly about this that I made a call to a friend of mine in the Department of Historic Resources and have already set in motion the initial steps, required by the State Review Board, to have the library declared a historical landmark."

Voices began to buzz. Billy jumped to his feet, his face scarlet, a large purple vein popping out on his neck. "You have no right to take this matter into your own hands! Who said you were in charge?"

"He can research whatever he wants!" shouted a voice, instigating increasingly heated comments from all quarters. Hoyt allowed this cacophony for about half a minute before he took action. "Sit down!" he roared across the din. "We're not going to accomplish anything with this racket! This is a public hearing, not a street brawl. There are still more people left on the docket who want to give their opinion."

"Actually, there is only one more person left to speak," said Reba. "Hiram Steinbacher? Are you here?"

Someone snickered and heads turned to look for the familiar scarecrow-like figure. But Hiram wasn't in the audience.

"I haven't seen him all day," said Reba Dove finally. "I went by the Brubaker place to put the dust covers on the furniture. Usually I see him working around the garden. Nevermind Billy tried to chase him off. He's as attached to this place as those big old trees out there.."

She called out again, "Will Hiram please come to the front of the room to address the audience?"

Jane leaned over and whispered, "I saw Hiram just yesterday, and he told me he couldn't wait to see the faces of some folks when he spoke at the meeting tonight."

Nanette piped up, "Well, I saw him down at Cootes' Store this morning getting some fertilizer for Bertha's garden. He seemed all right then!"

Hoyt stood up. "Since Hiram has failed to show up, this concludes our meeting. I'm convening a general information meeting next week. Professor Nelson has brought up an interesting twist to this whole new road project and the demolition of the library. I feel we need to continue to hear more about this proof he has and the results of the inquiries he made to the State Review Board."

"Another meeting?" Jacob Craun's thin, whining voice cut through the silence. "How many dang meetings do we need? Bunch of us here are willing and ready to sell our farms today!"

Hoyt glared at him. "I want every citizen in this town to feel she or he has had ample time to express opinions. We'll have as many meetings as it takes."

"How many more? You're just stalling for time, Hoyt. Easy to see whose side you're on!" came Craun's querulous voice again.

Hoyt closed his notebook, signaling that the conversation was over.

Marguerite waved her hand, hoping to catch Hoyt's attention over the din. "Mr. Chairman, if I may speak?"

Hoyt motioned for everyone to listen. Marguerite's fluted voice rang out across the room. "The Friends of the Library feel we have a vested interest in this outcome. We know the library serves a great purpose to our town. We have been gathering our own information and facts to validate the importance of the library to Custer's Mill. We would like a chance to present that information at the next meeting."

Nanette glared at Hoyt daring him to not take Marguerite's request seriously. Hoyt smiled. "Of course, Miss White. As I mentioned a few moments ago, I want every citizen of Custer's Mill to feel he or she has had a chance to express an opinion. We will make sure your name is on the docket. Now, do I have a motion to adjourn?"

The town meeting had been a fiasco. Darn that Professor Nelson, Billy thought, pounding both fists on the steering wheel. What a busybody!

Billy parked his car in the driveway at the Brubaker mansion, and turned off his headlights. Before he stepped out of the car, he leaned over and grabbed a flashlight from the glove compartment. A heavy shower had just passed through town, and only a sliver of a moon was visible in the cloudy night sky. Thunder rumbled in the distance.

Now that Aunt Bertha was gone, Billy felt a responsibility for making sure everything was in good order at the old place. Don't want any teenage hoodlums coming around to make trouble, he thought.

He breathed in a delightful aroma as he brushed past a few roses hanging over the pathway, wet with rainwater. His light shone on something red and blue beside the path. Must be something Hiram left out here, he thought. He stepped closer and focused the beam on the object. It was a work glove.

A sudden movement caused Billy to step backward into the nearby rosebush, snagging his pants on the thorns. His heart racing, he spoke sharply, "Who is it? Who's there?"

Billy lifted his flashlight to reveal muddy boots, then the familiar overalls and face of Hiram Steinbacher.

"Hiram, what the . . .? What are you doing here?"

"The wicked shall be turned into hell." Hiram spat out the words, and Billy took a step backward.

"Get out of here, Hiram! I told you I don't want you here anymore. Do I have to call the cops on you?" said Billy, his voice husky from fright and anger.

"Right," said Hiram, walking toward Billy. He stopped in the dim light and stared coldly at Billy for a long moment before moving off into the darkness of the garden. Billy shuddered involuntarily and watched him walk away. The familiar green van was parked behind the large boxwoods. Hiram backed out onto the driveway.

"Jerk," said Billy to himself as Hiram's taillights reached the gate. He wondered why Hiram had missed the town meeting. Billy bent to retrieve the glove lying in the pathway and shoved it in his pocket as he continued toward the house, deep in thought.

Chapter 26

"Come in, Emma." Pete sat at his desk, chin in his hands, smiling indulgently. Jake was behind him, looking at the floor.

"So you wanted to see me? That's what your message said." Emma's eyes were wary.

"So, Emma, sweetheart," Pete said, "me and Jake here are trying to figure out who's behind this little mishap at your townhouse."

"Someone threw a rock through my window with a threatening note attached. I don't call that a 'little mishap.'" Emma's voice rose in anger, despite her intent to remain calm. Pete had that effect on her.

"Well, I reckon we'll get to the bottom of it soon enough. Right, Jake? We're on the case!" Pete chuckled and prodded Jake with his elbow. "And now what's this I hear about you playing Miss Detective? That's our job, honey. Nosing around in people's business is the kind of thing that really stirs up a small town like ours, you know."

Jake shifted his weight and stared at a spot just over Emma's head, refusing to meet her gaze.

"Well, Pete," said Emma. "I have reason to believe Bertha had some secret to tell the town."

"Is that so?" said Pete, his smile bearing a trace of menace.

"Yes it is," answered Emma, avoiding Jake's sudden piercing stare.

"Well, whatever you think, you're causing trouble, for the town and the Brubaker family. So buzz off your little investigation. Leave these things to the professionals. Like us." He winked at Jake.

Emma responded with the barest of nods and locked eyes with Pete. He wouldn't get a word of agreement out of her, she thought.

Pompous ass! She looked at Jake, but once again he wouldn't meet her eyes. Hmm, thought Emma. So they're both just going to stonewall me. She'd see about that.

"We're working on the case, Emma," said Jake.

"I'm quite sure you're doing a wonderful job," responded Emma, her voice chilly and her expression even colder. "And now, it's time for me to get back to Aunt Mia's or she'll worry. So you have a nice evening, Jake, Pete."

Emma stalked out of the room. Jake stared after her, his jaw clenching and unclenching. Pete shrugged and began sorting through papers on the desk.

Jake followed Emma into the hallway. "Emma," he began. "Emma, you know—"

"Yes, I do know," Emma interrupted, turning to face him. "It's obvious where you stand on this."

"Emma," Jake tried again. "I have to do my job. That doesn't mean I don't have my own thoughts about things. You know I do."

"I have to go now," said Emma, angrily. "You should go hang out with your buddy Pete."

Jake looked hurt, then his eyes narrowed and his voice tightened.

"If that's how you want it, Emma," he said quietly. "But maybe it's time to question your own behavior instead of everybody else's. So long, Emma."

He turned and was gone. As Emma walked to her car, regret was already churning inside her. Her heart was heavy and she felt very alone.

So long, Jake.

Chapter 27

"Food for thought, ladies—literally!" Nanette took out pimento cheese sandwiches and began passing them out to the others. "We need some substance to be able to think better."

The Friends of the Library were gathered around the large oak table in the library's meeting room. The room doubled as a genealogy research space, and the walls were lined with bookshelves stuffed with volumes of family histories.

"Marguerite, you sure shocked me when you got up and told them we needed to have our say," Nanette said. "I was proud of you! I just hope our efforts won't be in vain."

"Why thank you Nanette, but I didn't see that we had any choice. I know the professor is doing all he can, but no one understands how important this library is to Custer's Mill as well as we do." The women nodded in agreement.

"If anybody can get the documentation we need to prove our library is a historical building, that brainy professor can!" said Nanette. "That's why he's off in Richmond doing research. I used to think he had too much book learning and no common sense. Now I'm beginning to think he just might have a little of both!"

"I'm sure he will do his best," Emma said. "If you need anything, just come and get me. The library's busy already, and we just opened." She looked around the table with great admiration. Jarrod Harmon might sport suits from Christian Dior, but these women were made of tough stuff. She, for one, would hate to come up against them.

The Friends of the Library worked through the morning, tabulating marks on half sheets of paper, counting up reference calls and adding the number of children participating in the summer reading program.

"I don't think we should include Internet use on the report. Might give the wrong impression." Nanette clamped her teeth down on the tip of her number-two lead pencil and frowned.

"Wrong impression of what?" Jane's eyes danced as she shoved a stack of papers toward her friend. "Here. Take a look at these numbers. We've had more computer use this week than in the past four weeks put together."

Nanette scowled. "I don't want the town to think that we're a host for the ungodly stuff that floats around out there in cyberspace or whatever they call it these days."

"I don't think the town holds us responsible for what our patrons do in the library. It's our job to provide a free informational service, not to censor knowledge." Jane stood up. "I, for one, am ready for a break. All of these numbers give me a headache. Anybody up for a walk around town?"

Nanette scowled. "I don't think so, Jane. We don't even have half of our presentation finished, and I don't want to work on it this weekend. Bella's due to lamb Saturday or Sunday and I need to be close by."

"Why don't you run out for a while, Jane? Nan and I can crunch these numbers." Marguerite gestured toward the door.

"I'll just hop down to the post office and check the library mail. I don't think Emma's picked it up yet this morning."

Nanette didn't even look up as Jane slipped out. "Forty-three reference calls? That sounds a bit high. I think Emma counts any call to the library as a reference call. Even if they just want to know if we're open."

"Technically, she's right," said Marguerite. "They are asking a question. Besides, we need all the ammunition we can get to throw at that slick-suited highway department man."

Nanette sighed. "Do you think we have a chance?" She pushed her reading glasses back up her nose and looked directly at her friend. "It's been my impression that what the government wants, the government gets. If they want our little library, I'm not sure there's a heck of a lot we can do about it."

116

"Nan, it's not like you to be so negative! Of course we can save the library. Old Albert's good for something besides his courtly manners. I'm sure he can find enough historical evidence to keep us afloat. Now's not the time to be blue, my dear."

"I know, Marguerite, but sometimes I just feel so old. When I see these young whippersnappers with their mobile phones and hear all of this talk about tweets and pings I realize just how ancient and outdated I am. Maybe nobody cares about an old library anymore."

"Chin up, old thing. We're not ready for the boneyard yet! We still have some mileage in these old skeletons. Let's get the details down on good old-fashioned paper. Now, how many young adult books were checked out last month?"

The women worked in silence for a half an hour, then Marguerite put down her pen. "This is good information. I'll ask Emma to make a PowerPoint for us to use Monday night."

"A power what?" Nanette stared at Marguerite.

"A PowerPoint, silly! A slide show!"

"Slide show? I don't even know what I did with my old thirty-five millimeter projector. It must be in the attic somewhere."

"Nanette, are you joking? A PowerPoint presentation runs on the computer, not a slide projector. Emma knows how to make the slide show, and I'm sure she would run it for us too. I think if we're going to impress those stuffed suits, we're going to have to step it up a notch. Give 'em some high-tech statistics to chew on."

Nanette looked doubtful. "I guess as long as we don't come across as some old fogies trying to look like they belong in the technology world."

"Trust me on this one, Nanette." Marguerite turned back to the pile of papers on the library table. "I know what I'm doing."

"That's a first!" came a slightly breathless voice from the doorway.

"Oh, she's back! Did you have a chance to stretch those old muscles of yours, Ms. Jane?"

"Whew! Am I ever out of shape!" Jane plopped down heavily on the wooden chair.

"Did you see anything exciting on your jaunt?" Nanette stood up and pushed both hands

"Not really. Unless you think a long line at the bank is exciting."

The door opened a second time, this time admitting the elderly professor.

"Well look who made it back from the big city!" Nanette grinned. "Tell us all you know, professor!"

Professor Nelson put down his briefcase and smiled.

"I believe we gathered some information that will astound our opponents and give everyone a good idea of what a valuable resource the library is to Custer's Mill," Nanette said as she pushed a yellow legal pad toward the newcomers.

Peering at Nanette's half sheet of paper with her tabulations, Professor Nelson gave a quiet whistle. "These are impressive numbers! I had no idea the library served so many people!"

"Impressive," agreed Jane, looking over his shoulder. "But a piece of paper is not the way to display these numbers."

"I know. Miss Smarty Pants, Marguerite, says we need a slide presentation." Nanette wrinkled her nose at her friend. "We're going to ask Emma to put it all together into a point power or something."

"PowerPoint, silly!"

Professor Nelson held up his hand. "If I may have your attention, ladies, let me tell what I've learned in Richmond. I still have some good contacts there."

"Of course you do," Jane said. "You know every historian south of the Mason-Dixon Line."

Professor Nelson bowed his head modestly. "When you have lived as many years as I have, you're bound to know a few people here and there." He took his glasses out of his shirt pocket and perched them low on his nose as he organized the papers in front of him. "Ladies, I am happy to say that we have completed the first step toward having our library declared a historic building. The fact that it was built in 1845, prior to the Civil War, and is an excellent example of the Federalist style, establishes that the building has architectural merit—one of the identifying factors that makes a building eligible for the National Registry."

"But is that enough?" inquired Marguerite. "You said it was the first step."

"Yes, but now we have to back up our claim with proof: documents that provide sufficient information for the State Review Board to deem the library worthy of historical significance."

"But Professor," Marguerite jumped in, "we have facts and figures on how many books are used and circulated each month, and we know we service a population area of over five thousand people. Those statistics we can find. But how are we going to get proof of what took place over 150 years ago?"

"It's an impossible task," said Nanette.

"Well, not as impossible as you may think, ladies. You just have to know where to look and what you are looking for. The fact that our library was once the town hall is important. Many of the town's oldest records are likely still in the basement vault. Over the years, the town council never got around to changing them over to microfiche. I believe that the original drawings for the building are down there, along with old records from the town including the Brubaker plantation. Why, there may even be the old census reports that show who owned slaves, and birth and death certificates. It will just take some digging."

Marguerite looked at the other ladies in astonishment. "We've always ignored that old basement. Not the most pleasant of places. Not to mention those rickety steps."

Professor Nelson frowned, but tried to remain positive. "Ladies, we'll have to find a way to get access to the vault. The future of our library is at stake. We must proceed with caution. Please, do not talk about the vault or our need for documents to anyone. The fewer people who know what we are doing the better!"

Chapter 28

"Looks like a full house." Aunt Mia held the door for Emma and both entered the town council building.

"I'm not sure if I want to sit beside the library ladies again," said Emma, as she scanned the back row to see if Jake was sitting there again. He wasn't. "Nanette never ceases to embarrass me with her offhand comments."

"Somebody taking my name in vain?" Nanette pushed past several people and put her hand on Emma's shoulder.

"I guess today's your time to shine, Nanette," Mia said to the older woman.

"Not me," Nanette scowled. She pointed accusingly to the other Friends of the Library, "They said I didn't know how to control my tongue. And—get this—that I would probably do more harm than good."

Emma held back a smile.

"So," said Jane, coming up behind her, "they picked the one who was used to trying to get the attention of an unenthusiastic crowd. Me! I guess they figured that after thirty years of teaching high school, I must have developed some sort of stage presence! I'm really kind of nervous, though. I hope our presentation is good enough."

"I think we did a great job, Jane. And it's not all on our shoulders. Other people are working on this." Emma walked with the group toward the front. "Don't worry about the technology part. Just give me a nod when you're ready to change the slide."

Hoyt began the meeting and called Professor Nelson to the stand. Emma gave her uncle a thumbs-up. He touched his beret in response as he walked toward the podium.

"Thank you, Chairman. Ladies and gentlemen, at the last meeting I presented my expectations that our library has historical merit. I now can tell you that based on the age of the building and its historical significance to the Civil War, the Department of Historical Resources has established that our library would qualify to be listed on the National Registry of Historical Landmarks."

The audience grew restless. Shep stood. "Well, what good is that going to do all of us? You said you were watching out for our best interests? Well I think the best interest of this town would be to take down that old building and get us some business in here. We can always build a new library out in the county somewhere." People began talking all at once and Hoyt rapped the gavel and tried to bring order back to the room.

"Shep Crawford, you are out of order. You had a chance to sign up and speak, but your name's not on the list. Right now, Professor Nelson has the floor."

The professor looked out over the audience with a forced smile. "I, for one, want to preserve our valuable heritage. Let the record show I plan to gather the necessary documents for the library building to be officially listed on the National Registry." With this, the professor took his seat, and Jacob Craun moved to the front of the room.

"You know I'm a man of few words." The farmer's voice was high-pitched. "I'm for the new road and selling off whatever land they need to build it. I want the money and am happy to take it! I don't think you should let the professor here put these notions in your heads that this library is more important than feeding your families. That's all I got to say." Craun took his seat to the sound of loud clapping and a few "Wahoos!" Obviously others felt as he did.

Finally, it was time for the Friends of the Library to speak. With one last look at her colleagues for moral support, Jane stepped to the front of the room.

"I must say I haven't stood in front of most of you for quite a few years—probably since your last geology class," she began. A few members of the audience smiled as they remembered Jane's science class.

121

"Some of you probably thought that after you graduated from high school you wouldn't have to listen to my lectures anymore. But here I am, and there you are!"

"Just get on with it!" came a querulous voice from the middle of the room.

Jane took a deep breath and began to explain in detail how the community used the library as Emma supported her words with the PowerPoint slides. She did her best to clarify the numbers and charts they had put together, but the audience shuffled in their seats. The numbers were failing to charm. Jane raised her voice to try to combat the noise of the squeaking chairs. "And as you can see, we have quite an impressive usage of our computers each week, and this year's book circulations are up by 20 percent over last year's."

Shep called out from the audience, "I seen a bunch of figures that don't amount to a hill of beans. It ain't enough to convince us to keep this old building. I say we let the transportation department bring in the new road and tear down that library!"

Jane's normally mild temper had reached a boiling point. She walked down the aisle and stood in front of the heckler, her voice calm but full of passion. "Shep Crawford, you'll be singing a different tune when we get those documents out of the vault in the library basement! The professor says there are drawings, old records, and all kinds of official papers we can use as proof. Why, we will have all the proof we need when we get into that vault."

The audience erupted into shouts, and Emma turned to see her uncle moving toward the door. It was then that she noticed Jake standing in the back of the room. Their eyes met for just a second. Then Emma turned her attention to Jane.

Jane had slumped down in the nearest chair, exhausted and humiliated. Emma turned off the projector.

Her face was grim. The meeting might be over, but the fallout was just beginning.

Chapter 29

The wind ruffled the corners of Hiram's note as it lay on the seat next to Jake. He didn't use the air conditioner in the cruiser unless the temperature hit at least ninety degrees. Fresh air, even if it was hot, always revived his senses and sharpened his brain. It didn't take long for Jake to find the trailer park at the end of Elm Street. The U.S. Postal Service had no real address for Hiram; Jake had checked, but Pete had directed him to start at Sissy Lambert's place.

He was in luck. The green van rested at the end of a gravel drive beside the trailer. The hood of the Green Hornet was propped up with a piece of firewood, and Hiram's head was buried under the metal roof. Jake turned off the ignition, picked up the note, and walked toward the older man.

"Nice day," Jake said to what he could see of Hiram.

Hiram continued to pound the battery cables as though Jake hadn't spoken. Jake cleared his throat and tried again. "Mr. Steinbacher, could we talk for a few minutes?" Jake had folded the note in his hand so it wasn't obvious. Hiram was watching him out of the corner of his eye, but he had made no attempt to direct his attention away from the battery.

"Excuse me, Mr. Steinbacher. I really would like to talk with you for a few minutes."

This time, Hiram pulled his head out from under the hood and stared at Jake.

"It's Hiram. Just call me Hiram." He took a grubby handkerchief from his back pocket and began to wipe the grease off his hands.

Jake extended his hand as a peace offering. "Okay, Hiram, I'm Jake Preston, the new county detective. I've seen you around, but we haven't been formally introduced."

"Yeah, I know who you are. I reckon you've come to talk to me about Miss Bertha. Figured you'd get here sooner or later. What's taken you so long?"

Jake was a little surprised by Hiram's abruptness.

"Yes, I have a few questions for you, Hiram, about Miss Bertha Brubaker. I understand you worked as her gardener. When was the last time you saw her alive?"

Although Jake listened carefully for Hiram's response, he also watched the older man's face. Sometimes Jake could tell a lot more from a person's body language than what they revealed in words.

Hiram looked down, and moved a small pile of gravel with the toe of his boot. He took a minute or two before he answered. "I saw her that Monday when I was workin' in the rose garden. Twenty-five years I worked for Miss Bertha . . . she trusted me. Not like that snivelin' little weasel of a nephew of hers who never did nothin'." Hiram stood up straight and looked up toward the sky. His voice rang out clear and strong. "He who sins is of the devil, for the devil has been sinning from the beginning!"

Jake wasn't sure what connection the Scripture had to his question. He had already heard Hiram's biblical rantings and warnings at Bertha's funeral. "This note was found in Miss Brubaker's things, Hiram. Why did you send this to her and what does it mean?" Jake held out the note.

Hiram wouldn't take the paper, but stepped closer to Jake. He looked deep into Jake's eyes, as if sizing up his very soul. "I thought she should be careful. I told her there was evil lurking around. The eyes of the Lord are in every place, keeping watch on the evil and the good."

Jake tried to analyze the abrupt shifts in Hiram's behaviors and responses. He wasn't convinced Hiram was as eccentric as the townsfolk thought. He was just about to ask Hiram what enemies he felt lurked around Bertha Brubaker, when the door of the trailer opened and a young woman stepped out on the porch.

"Daddy, is everything okay? Is there something wrong, Officer?" Sissy came quickly to stand at her father's side. "Hello. I'm Sissy Lambert. Is there something wrong?" There was a note of concern in her voice.

"No, ma'am! I don't think we've met. I'm Jake Preston, the new county detective. I just had a few questions for your father. I understand he saw Miss Bertha Brubaker on the day she died."

"Well, maybe he did, but he doesn't know anything about Miss Bertha's death. He took Miss Bertha's death real hard. She was real good to my daddy and she always said nobody took care of her flowers like 'Old Hiram.' Isn't that right Daddy?" Sissy had positioned herself between Jake and Hiram, ready to protect her father if necessary.

"Well, that's what I've heard, but I needed to come by and ask for myself. You understand. Besides, this note from your father was found in Miss Brubaker's belongings after her death." Jake unfolded the paper and handed it to Sissy.

Sissy read the note carefully, as if she hadn't seen it before. "My daddy likes to quote the Bible. He's always doing things like that. I don't think he meant anything by this. Sissy handed the note back to Jake.

"I've said all I have to say, Officer," said Hiram.

"Well, like I said, I needed to come by and check on this. Thanks for your time, ma'am, sir." Jake walked back toward his car. He could hear the crunch of gravel and knew Hiram was following him.

"I wasn't the only one workin' in the garden that day." Hiram stopped in the middle of the driveway. Jake turned to face him. "Miss Bertha had that Shep Crawford there helpin' me, just like she had him there when we did the spring planting. I told her I don't need no help, but she insisted. Shep Crawford's the one you need to talk to. I tried to warn her about him and the others." The two men stared at each other for a minute.

"What others, Hiram?"

Hiram walked back to his truck without answering, and Jake finally turned toward the street.

Jake sat in his cruiser and looked up Shep Crawford's address. It was Jenkins Hollow Road. way out in the county. He edged the car out of

125

Sissy's drive and down Main Street. Jake hadn't been in that part of the county yet, but this seemed like as good a time as any. Besides, he was intrigued by Hiram's last comments. Funny. No one had mentioned that Shep Crawford was at the Brubaker estate on that Monday.

Despite the trouble brewing in town, the day was lovely. Glad to be free from the confines of city streets and rows of houses, he rolled down all four windows of the car and turned up the stereo. He had to take his rest breaks when he could get them. Determined not to think of the case until he reached Jenkins Hollow Road, Jake began to hum along with Bruce Springsteen, quietly at first, and then at full volume as the cruiser picked up speed.

Nobody alive today could remember the last time anyone by the name of Jenkins had lived in Jenkins Hollow. The last family bearing that surname moved West just after the Civil War. Before they left, they sold their farm and the surrounding woodlands to Abel Dove, who had hired Criders, Lamberts, and Crawfords as farmhands. In the years that followed, several other families moved into the hollow, but no one bothered to change the name.

Shep Crawford and his grandmother lived near a sharp turn in the road. Jake was beginning to wonder if the rocky path he was traveling even qualified as a road. He'd put the cruiser in four-wheel drive right after he had left the paved stretch and now, even the tug of all four wheels didn't seem to create enough leverage to propel him over the washboard lane.

He was almost ready to park the car and continue his journey on foot when he noticed a clearing ahead. A small brown house leaned toward the northeast as though a continuous southwest wind was pushing it in that particular direction. The narrow two-rooms-up, two-rooms-down structure was covered in weather-beaten siding, its rough surface blending with the woods that hovered close by.

When Jake was a young boy, he had always thought that someday the forest would grow back over the acres of land that had been clear-cut—that the earth would once more be a tangle of brambles, brush, and trees, swallowing all traces of asphalt and steel. The woods loomed near the old Crawford place as if waiting for someone to slack off, to forget to mow the thick crabgrass or neglect to keep the wild rose bushes trimmed. That would be the chink in the armor, the cue to move in. To reclaim.

Although the front porch was sagging and the board across the threshold was split, Jake noticed that the front steps had recently been replaced with sturdy, pressure-treated wood. At least he wouldn't fall through, he thought with a wry smile. If only Mirabelle could see him now. She had always laughed at his citified manners and his complete lack of understanding of Southern country folks. Being born in Boston did have its drawbacks to understanding the finer points of Appalachian culture, he admitted to himself.

He rapped on the wooden frame surrounding a torn screen door. "Anybody home?"

"Well, if it ain't the lawman." Shep leaned against the door and held it halfway open. "Reckon you might as well come in."

Jake walked into the small, dark space. Although the temperature outside had reached the upper seventies, a crackling fire burned in the woodstove in the center of the room. The windows were shut, and aside from the thin breeze that came through the rips in the screen door, there was no air stirring. Jake fought a sudden flash of claustrophobia.

"Little stuffy in here. But the Granny, she likes it warm. Don't you, Gran?"

The diminutive, wizened woman sitting in the corner stared at her grandson with small, dark, bead-like eyes, but didn't say a word.

Jake nodded. "Well, I won't keep you long. I just need to ask you a couple of questions about Miss Bertha and how well you and your grandmother knew her."

Shep pointed to a small, cane-bottomed chair. "Sit a spell. Let me get you a drink."

Jake was about to refuse when he realized that a cold drink might help combat the stifling heat of the room. He nodded, but immediately regretted his decision when Shep reached to the floor beside his chair and pulled a warm cola from a cardboard box. He popped the top and handed it to Jake.

"Now, I don't know what it is you want to know about me and Miss Bertha, but I'll warn you right now, there ain't much to tell."

A skinny beagle mutt came in from the side room and eyed Jake curiously. "It's all right, Butcher. This here's the Law. He won't hurt you." The dog took a step closer to Jake and growled. Shep muttered something under his breath and the dog backed away.

"I know that Miss Bertha sometimes had you help Hiram with the spring planting. Did you work in her garden this year?"

Shep's nod was noncommittal. "I put some seeds in the ground for her. Hiram don't want no help. He don't like me messing with his plants. But sometimes Miss Bertha just gets—got—it in her head that Hiram needed an extra set of hands."

"Do you remember if you were at the Brubaker estate four weeks ago?"

Shep narrowed his eyes and looked at Jake. "You mean was I down there when she died? What is this? You think I had something to do with her dying?"

Mrs. Crawford began to rock back and forth on her chair.

"See, you done went and disturbed the Granny. It's okay, Gran. Just sit back and relax. This lawman is just about ready to head back down the hill."

Jake smiled at the old woman. "I'm sorry, Mrs. Crawford. I didn't mean to disturb you."

The rocking slowed slightly and she fixed her beady eyes on Jake. "Old sins cast long shadows," she said in a soft, rasping voice.

"Ma'am?" Jake leaned forward and waited for her to continue her conversation, but Bessie Crawford had closed her eyes and appeared to be asleep.

Jake took a sip of the tepid soda and his stomach lurched. He had to get out of this suffocating room. "Shep, you think about your last visit to Miss Bertha, and we'll talk again. Maybe you can look me up the next time you come into town for groceries?"

"Might not be until the day after tomorrow." Shep scratched the stubble on his grizzled chin. "Maybe not till the day after that."

"Just as long as we can talk in the next couple of days that will be fine." Jake stood up.

"Course, Officer. Nothin' I'd like better than another stimulatin' conversation with you."

Shep held the rickety door open wide and ushered Jake out with a dramatic sweep of his arm.

Chapter 30

Emma hadn't noticed the numbers until now. The series of six numbers were scrawled along the upper margin in the month of February and she had been focusing her attention only on the May and June pages. Today, however she had decided to start at the beginning of the pile of copied pages and do a systematic study of the contents. And there they were—a mysterious series of numbers lined up along the top of the page for the first day of February—12-13-37. Could they possibly be the combination to the Brubaker vault? There weren't enough numbers to make up a telephone listing. Emma felt a shiver of excitement run down her spine. She had to go to the vault and try the numbers. Right now.

The library wasn't scheduled to open for another hour. She had time. Pulling on her sweater and grabbing her cell phone, Emma opened the basement door and looked down into the darkness. For a moment she hesitated. Should she let someone know she was going to attempt to get into the vault? Should she call Jake? She dismissed these thoughts almost as soon as they crossed her mind. Marguerite and Nanette would be here soon anyway.

Emma descended the stairs. The musty scent of old paper and damp earth rose to meet her as her feet touched the cool cement floor of the basement. She flipped a switch and a thin ray of light shone from the cobwebbed beams above. The vault door was in the shadows and she could just make out the shape of the tumbler lock. She was going to need more light. Next time, she'd remember to bring the penlight from her desk. Emma walked closer, letting the light from her phone play over the wall. She could make out a series of long, triangular points placed in a circular pattern. Was it some sort of symbol?

"Curiouser and curiouser," muttered Emma, feeling like Alice in Wonderland. Emma took a tissue from her sweater pocket and began to wipe away the dust. Much of the grime was ingrained and would take a lot of scrubbing to come clean, but she was able to uncover a faint fleur-de-lis marking at the top. She snapped a picture of the symbol with her cell phone camera. I hope the flash works for this, she thought. I want Uncle Albert to see it.

She took a closer look at the tumbler lock. Bright lines of brass showed through large gashes cut into the surface of the lock. Somebody had tried to get into the vault without benefit of a combination. Recently. Emma shivered.

She tried several groupings of the series of numbers she'd found in Bertha's planner, but the lock remained firmly in place. If these were the correct numbers, she had the wrong sequence.

Emma heard the back door open and the voices of her library volunteers floated down the stairs. She sighed.

If only Miss Bertha hadn't taken so many secrets to the grave.

Chapter 31

"Ali! Ali! Ali! Ali!" Kate bounced up and down like a hyperactive jumping bean as her young babysitter opened the front door.

"Hey, Kit Kat! What's up? Why so bouncy? Pretending you're Tigger again?"

"It's better'n that! Daddy said that you could take me to the park today!"

Ali looked at Jake, eyes wide. "That true, Mr. Preston? You trust me to take Kit Kat to the park?"

"Should I?" Jake looked at her in mock seriousness. "Do you think you're ready for such a mission?"

Ali drew herself up to her full five feet and tilted her chin upward. "Sure, Mr Preston. You can count on me. First, we'll go by the library for story time and then go to the park. That sound good?"

Jake picked up his lunch box and car keys from the kitchen table. "Miss Kate forgot an important part of this scenario. What did you leave out, Kate?"

Kate lowered her eyes. "Gotta do my chores first," she mumbled.

"Yes ma'am! Feed Delphinium, clean her litter box, and make your bed." Jake made tick marks in the air as though checking off a list.

"Daaaaddy!" Kate drawled. "I know what I have to do. You don't have to remind me!" She stood, hands on hips, tapping her right foot in her classic Minnie Mouse pose . . . Minnie Mouse and Mirabelle. He felt a lump rise in his throat. Kate's mother had had the same stance when she was upset with him for some misdemeanor. Jake suddenly scooped his daughter up into his arms and held her tightly.

"Daddy," she squirmed, "you're squeezing me to death!"

"Sorry, sweetie." He set her gently on the floor. "Just giving you a goodbye hug, that's all."

"Bye, Daddy!"

The girls watched Jake pull out of the driveway and take off down the street.

"Well, Kit Kat, you start your chores and I'll straighten up the kitchen. What do you think?" The twangy sound of country music filled the air. "Oh, my phone! Like my new ringtone?"

Kate wrinkled her nose. "No. I can't stand that kind of music!"

But Ali was already talking to the person on the other end of the line.

"Oh, hey, Kirsten! Yeah, I'm with Kit Kat today. No, I can't guess. Who did you see? Who?"

Kate rearranged some school papers on the kitchen table and stared at Ali. "You did what? Kirsten!" Ali was saying. "That's dumb! You should've asked me first! I don't care what he said. You're a horrible friend! No, I don't want to talk about it." Ali put the phone back in her jeans pocket only to have the ringtone blare out again. "What!" Ali almost yelled into the phone. "Yeah, we're going to the library after a while. Why? I'm not sure I want to talk to you. Maybe." This time when she hung up the phone didn't ring again.

"You mad at Kirsten?" Kate twirled a strand of hair around her finger and looked at Ali quizzically.

"None of your beeswax, Kit Kat. But since I'm a nice person, unlike some other people I know, I will tell you anyway. Kirsten is talking to Bobby."

"That's it?" Kate looked incredulous. "I talk to Bobby and you don't get mad at me!"

"That's different. You're a little kid. Now, I'm done talking about her. Grab your books and let's head out to the library."

"And the park!" Kate ran to get her backpack.

"Hi, girls," Emma smiled as Kate plopped her backpack on the counter.

"Hi, Miss Emma! Do you have a new book for me today?"

"You betcha. Take a look at this." Emma pulled a book from the shelf behind the desk.

"It's a lamb!" Kate squealed. "I saw the lambs on Miss Nanette's farm! With my 4-H club!" She held the book in both hands and smiled up at Emma. "Will you read it to me?"

Emma scanned the library. Her new volunteer, Lula Parker, was shelving books, Marguerite was changing the pictures on the bulletin board, and Jane could handle checkouts for a few minutes. "Sure, Kate. Just sit down over there on the purple sofa by the window. I'll be there as soon as I find Miss Jane."

Kate and Emma snuggled together on the sofa and began to read. Behind them, near the back of the library, Ali and Kirsten talked in loud whispers.

"Miss Emma, you know what?"

"What, Kate?"

"I'm glad I'm not a teenager."

Emma followed her gaze to the two girls glaring at each other across the table. "Me too." The girls' voices rose in agitation and then fell back into whispers.

Emma had just finished reading the story when Ali came to get Kate. Kirsten trailed unhappily behind her.

"Come on, Kit Kat Kate. We need to get on to the park before it's too late."

Emma took the book to the desk, checked it out, and stuffed it into Kate's pink backpack. She waved goodbye as they walked out the door.

The park was nearly empty. Kate tossed her backpack on the ground and ran toward the swings. Ali and Kirsten sat at opposite ends of the stone park bench. Staring straight ahead, they ignored their young charge.

Kate set the swing in motion with a big push. Within seconds, she was gliding higher and higher.

"Ali! Kirsten! Look how high I can swing!" Kate called out to the teens only to have her voice fall on deaf ears.

From the edge of the park, a man stood watching. His face was hidden by a dark hoodie, and his black jeans blended into shadows.

A twig snapped and Kate turned her head toward the sound. Suddenly, a strong arm circled her waist, pulling her from the swing.

Kate screamed. The stranger clamped a gloved hand over her mouth, muffling her cries. He hissed into her ear. "What are you doing here? I'm gonna make sure you and your daddy don't mess things up!"

Kirsten and Ali looked up just in time to see the stranger pulling Kate from the swing. They screamed and ran toward the hooded man.

Lisa Benedict hadn't planned on conducting a rescue mission. In fact, if her black lab hadn't needed exercise, she'd be at home reading on her day off. One more lap around the park and she'd head back. It was then that she heard the screams. Instinctively, she reached down and released the lab's leash.

The dog ran straight toward the swings. And then Lisa saw the child. "Attack, Rex!"

That was all the instruction the dog needed. Running at full speed, Rex sent the man tumbling to the ground. The jolt was enough for the kidnapper to release his hold. The child broke free and ran sobbing toward the Lisa and the two girls.

A siren wailed in the distance.

Chapter 32

Jake pulled his police car into the lot next to the swings and jumped out, turning the siren off, but leaving the blue light flashing. He saw Ali bending over Kate. Calling out as he ran toward them, a sense of dread began to chill his heart. "A call came through about a child abduction here. What's going on, Ali? Is Kate okay?"

As soon as she heard her father's voice, Kate leapt up and raced to meet him. Tears and dirt streaked down her face. Jake looked from Kate to Kirsten to Ali and then to the stranger with the dog. He held Kate in a tight hug, and felt her body trembling. "What is it, honey? Tell me what's happened."

The words tumbled from Ali's mouth. "There was a man and we didn't see him. I should have paid more attention to Kate. We were sitting on the bench over there..." her voice trailed off, and Kirsten took up the story.

"This lady's dog saved Kate." The black lab stared at Jake with large, dark eyes, his tongue lolling to one side.

"I made the call, Officer," said the woman. "I saw a man in dark clothes running away with this little girl here—Kate. Is she your daughter? It all happened so fast. When the girls screamed, I saw him dragging her away so I unleashed Rex. He's well-trained and big enough to scare most people. He was barking like crazy, though. Anyway, Rex jumped on the man and knocked him over, and the little girl was able to wriggle out of his grip." The woman pointed to a stand of tall oak trees that ringed the playground. "The man took off over there behind those trees, down the alley." She smiled at Kate. "I think she's badly shaken, but not hurt, thank God."

Jake's mind was reeling. Was there a child molester in Custer's Mill? No other reports of child abductions had been reported in the area. Why would someone want to harm Kate?

Jake held Kate close to him as he walked to his car in long, rapid strides. He needed to call this in right away so the area could be searched, although he knew the perpetrator was likely far away by now.

Everything seemed surreal to him. It was as though he was watching himself from a distance. Was this really happening? He swung the car door open wide so he could put his legs on the ground and settle Kate on his lap. He gently rocked her and felt her trembling subside. "Honey, please, tell me . . . are you all right?"

Kate turned her tear-stained face to her father and looked into his eyes. Jake felt a crushing anger wash over him. Whoever had done this to her would pay.

"He told me that you and me, we shouldn't be here, Daddy." Kate's voice was soft, so unlike her usual confident tone. "He said he was gonna make sure we didn't mess things up. I think he wanted to hurt me, Daddy, and I was so scared!"

"Kate," said Jake, "I need to talk to these people. Come with me now, okay? You're my brave girlie, Kate." She nodded, then stood up and took her father's hand. They walked back toward the woman and her dog and the babysitters, all waiting at the edge of the parking lot.

Jake could feel his heart beating wildly. How could this be happening? He had such hopes for their new life, starting over in Custer's Mill. He struggled to calm himself and focus on his duties as an officer. "Ma'am, thank you for your quick action! You probably saved my daughter's life." Jake reached out to shake the woman's hand. He patted Rex on the head. "And thank you too, Rex. Now if you don't mind, I need to ask you all a few questions." He flipped open his notebook. "First, may I have your name and contact information?"

"Lisa Benedict, Officer. And I live—"

Just then, screeching tires diverted the attention of the group as The Custer's Mill police chief pulled up in the lot and swung his car around with a jerk. "I got your call and came here as fast as I could. There's been a kidnapping?"

"*Attempted* kidnapping." Jake squeezed Kate's hand. "This woman saved Kate. Her dog frightened the abductor and chased him away. I was just taking her statement."

"Let me do that, Jake." Pete took in the little group of shaken witnesses. "This crime happened here in our town, on our watch, so I'll take over from here. You need to get your daughter home and try to get her settled down. I'll let you know how things are going."

"Thanks, Pete! I owe you."

Rex jumped up and licked Kate's face, making her giggle. Jake was grateful for the distraction. He thanked Lisa again, spoke a few quiet words to Ali and Kirsten, and insisted on dropping the two teens off at the library.

He ushered the girls into the police car and surprised himself with the presence of mind to make them all buckle their seat belts. He wouldn't be able to forgive himself if anything happened to Kate. As he started the engine, he turned his head to glance at her, small and forlorn, in the center of the backseat.

His precious daughter was safe—for now.

Chapter 33

"You two look like you've seen a ghost!" Emma looked up from the computer and smiled as Ali burst through the library door, followed by Kirsten.

"It was absolutely horrible! Terrible! The worst thing I've ever seen!" Ali put her head on the checkout counter and burst into tears.

"Hey, what's wrong? I didn't mean to upset you." Emma put her hand on the young girl's shoulder.

"He just grabbed her! Just like that! Then he took off running! If it hadn't been for that lady and her dog . . ." Ali erupted into a fresh sob.

Emma felt a chill run down her spine. "Who grabbed whom? Is everybody okay? Ali, you have to calm down and tell me exactly what happened." She got a bottle of water from her lunch box and handed it to the weeping girl. "Here, drink this and take a deep breath."

Ali took a long drink of water, hiccupped and grabbed a tissue from the box on the desk. "We were in the park. Kirsten and Kate and me . . ."

"Kate?" Emma's voice was sharper than she had intended.

"We were babysitting her. Or we were supposed to be. Kirsten was dumb enough to agree to go to the dance with Bobby when she knew good and well that I was just waiting for the right time to ask him myself."

"Ali, please. We can talk about your boy troubles later. What about Kate? Is she okay?"

"She is now. Some person—a man, I think—just came out of nowhere and pulled her off the swing and started running away with her."

Emma gasped.

"And then this woman let her dog loose and he chased the man. The man dropped Kate and ran."

"Does Jake know?" Emma struggled to keep her voice calm.

"Yeah, he came when the lady called 911."

"Girls, we're going to close the library early today." Emma was already shutting down the computer. "You walk through the aisles and make sure there is no one still here."

Emma turned the lights out and walked outside with Ali and Kirsten. "You go on home now. I have an important errand to run."

"Gonna go see Jake?" The question was an innocent one, but the look Ali gave Emma was sly.

"I want to check on Kate," said Emma briskly. "I need to make sure she's all right."

"Sure. Whatever you say!" The girls headed down the sidewalk leaving Emma to wonder where Ali got her ideas about her and Jake. Oh the joys of living in a small town!

Jake was wearing a pink flowered apron over his police uniform when he answered the door. He blushed when he saw Emma. "Not my usual getup, I assure you."

"Pink is definitely your color." Emma smiled. "But I'm actually here on serious business. How's she doing? Ali told me."

Jake looked grim. "Sleeping now. The drama wore her out. You might as well come in." He held the door wider, and Emma walked inside. The tiny living room was cluttered with what appeared to be the castoffs of a serious entomologist. A butterfly net was propped against the sofa, several jars with holes lined the small bookshelf, and a brown paper bag labeled "Don't you dare touch" sprawled on the floor.

"I apologize for the mess," said Jake as he cleared off a space for Emma to sit. "Kate is into bugs now. Says they're the new way to cure world hunger."

Jake picked up a sleeping ball of fur and placed it gently on the floor. The kitten protested with a loud mew. "Sorry, Delphinium. I need a place to sit too."

Emma looked past Jake, through the small bay window and into the street. Somewhere out there in the tiny town of Custer's Mill a kidnapper lurked. And not just a kidnapper. A cold-blooded killer.

She shivered.

"Are you cold? I can turn the fan off." He pointed to a small, round machine that seemed to be merely recirculating the stuffy air.

"No, I'm not cold. I'm just scared. And sorry."

"Sorry?" Jake raised an eyebrow.

"Oh, stop pretending, Jake. You know I was mad at you the other day at the station. Seemed like you were taking Pete's side. And I guess you might already realize I can be pretty mean when I think things are unfair." Her voice trailed off.

"You've had a lot of stress lately, Emma." Jake's voice was tired. "We all have, with Miss Bertha's death, the threat to the library, a break-in at your house, and now Kate's close call. Something's gotta give soon. We can't keep going on like this."

"Have you talked to Pete? Does he have any ideas?"

Jake didn't answer at first, and when he did, he spoke slowly as though he were forming his thoughts as he said them aloud. "I think Pete is a little overwhelmed. I get the impression that he hasn't had to deal with any serious crimes here in Custer's Mill. Things had been generally quiet until now. He did say he'd give Kate's attempted kidnapping his full attention. But I'm not so sure he knows what to do."

"Well then, he should let you handle it."

"This will be a State Police investigaion—kidnapping's a big deal. But I do intend to look into it myself as well."

"How many people have to be endangered before he takes his job more seriously?" Emma's voice rose and Jake glanced down the hallway toward Kate's bedroom door.

Emma clamped a hand over her mouth. "Oh, I'm so sorry! I hope I didn't wake her!"

"She sleeps pretty sound. I doubt you even fazed her."

Emma rose. "I have to go. I just wanted to make sure Kate was all right. And you. Are you okay too?" Now that they both stood up, there was very little distance between them in the cramped living room.

"I'm fine, Emma," he said softly. Their eyes locked. "Thanks for coming."

"Daddy!" came a small voice from the back bedroom. "Daddy!"

Emma pulled her gaze away. "I'll be going now. Give her a hug for me!"

The angle of the sun highlighted the chipped paint on the old farmhouse table as Nanette poured thick, dark liquid into Jane and Marguerite's cracked mugs. "Just like that? He tried to take her in broad daylight?" Nanette set the pot down with a thud. "How'd he think he could get away with it?"

"Technically, he did get away," said Marguerite, eyeing the contents of her cup warily. "What's this, Nanette? Coffee? Tea? Cyanide?"

"Bergamot. Grew it in the garden this year. It's the stuff in Earl Grey. Figured it might taste okay on its own. You know, without all of the other stuff they add to tea these days."

Jane swirled her cup and looked at the brown water as if hoping that perhaps some of the "other stuff" might be added after all.

"Yes, he got away. And if it's up to that lazy Pete Anderson to find the guy, I have a feeling the creep's home free." Nanette set a sugar bowl on the table and both Jane and Marguerite reached for it.

"Well, I think that new detective, Jake Preston, will be on it. He seems sharp enough. And besides, I don't think he'll trifle with a man who tried to kidnap his daughter."

"Why Kate?" Jane tentatively sipped her tea and quickly set the cup back down on the table. "I don't think Detective Preston is unduly wealthy. They certainly couldn't be after money."

Marguerite shook her head. "I don't like the looks of recent events here in Custer's Mill. First, some bigwig from the highway department threatens to destroy our library, then Miss Bertha is poisoned, and now Kate is almost kidnapped. At first glance, there doesn't seem to be a connection among these events. But it's been my experience that so many tragic happenings must be linked in some way—especially if their origins appear to be somewhat mysterious"

"More tea, ladies?" Nanette held up the teapot.

Jane and Marguerite shook their heads in unison and pulled their mugs out of Nanette's reach.

"Well, I don't like it," said Marguerite. "And I don't like the fact that Detective Preston has middle school girls looking after Kate. I know they mean well, but what can fourteen-year-old girls do in a crisis?"

"Maybe we should volunteer to take turns watching her," said Jane. "At least through the summer. I'm sure it will be easier for Detective Preston once school starts."

"Good idea," Nanette said. "Marguerite, maybe you can work up a schedule. I know Kate will have a blast here on the farm. And I suppose," she said, narrowing her eyes, "that you two old trouts will find a way to entertain her too."

Marguerite huffed. "I'm sure Kate will enjoy her time with us as well, Nanette. There's certainly more to life than scooping manure and growing bergamot."

Chapter 34

"Are you sure you're okay with this, Emma?"

"With what? Having Jake over for dinner? Of course! Why wouldn't I be?"

Mia smiled. "You just seem to be a little confused on how you feel about him, that's all. And I thought he might enjoy a relaxing evening after all the stress of Kate's trauma this week."

"There's not much I'm clear about these days." Emma sighed and plopped a newspaper down onto the table. "Look what I found."

The *Custer's Mill Star* was yellow with age. The print was fading and the photos grainy, but the headline was clear: "Fire Claims Life of Custer's Mill Citizen."

"What have we here?" Mia touched the page lightly. "Oh, I remember this! What a tragedy! You know, the woman killed would have been Jake's former mother-in-law."

"I know. That's why the article struck me. Is Jake just doomed to a string of bad luck or is there a pattern in all of this disaster? First, Kath dies in a fire. Then her daughter, Jake's wife, is killed in a freak auto accident. And now, Kate is almost kidnapped. What's the deal?"

"How did you come across this article, Emma?"

"I was going through some old newspapers trying to find information that would help document the history of the library building, and I saw the headline. I guess I was too young to remember the fire."

Mia set a plate of deviled eggs on the table and paused to look out the window. "I was a senior in high school when it happened. I still remember the smoky smell. It hung in the air for days."

The doorbell rang and both women jumped. "We're a nervous lot," said Mia. "Can you get the door?"

"What? No Kate?" Emma was genuinely disappointed when she saw Jake standing alone on the doorstep.

"Well isn't that a greeting to boost a man's ego!" Jake grinned. "I wasn't about to let her out of my sight, but then Nanette stopped by and offered to show her how to knit. With her own homegrown alpaca yarn. Kate was so mesmerized I couldn't pull her away. Funny how those two have taken to each other. Nanette's going to take her out for supper. I have to admit, I'm a little nervous about being away from her."

Mia set a steaming platter of barbequed ribs on the table. Emma moved the old newspaper out of the way.

"Research?" Jake nodded toward the newspaper.

Emma tried to move the paper out of sight before Jake reached for it. Too late. He picked it up and read the headline. "Fire Claims Life of Custer's Mill Citizen." He gave Emma a curious glance, but his tone conveyed a note of threat.

"What are you doing with this article?"

"Well, I just . . ." Emma stammered. "I'm sorry, Jake, I know this is . . ." Her voice trailed off.

"This is the fire that killed my mother-in-law. But why do you have it? You're not connecting this with current events, are you?"

Emma shook her head, avoiding Jake's eyes. "I just came across it while I was researching the age of our library building." She brightened. "But if you're interested, we could do more research on this *and* on the building at the library. Unless it's too painful for you. "

Jake sat silently, staring at the faded newspaper. "It's not painful, Emma. My wife was just a toddler when her mother died. Still . . ." He paused. "If you'll show me how to work the microfiche, I'd like to do some research of my own on this."

"Sure. Tomorrow's Sunday. Want to meet after church? You can bring Kate and I'll let her see some new books we just got in...all about bugs. She'll love that."

"That sounds like a wonderful plan, folks," said Mia briskly. "Now, let's put all thoughts of the past and future out of our heads and concentrate on the present. The spare ribs are getting cold!"

145

"You don't have to tell me twice," said Jake, piling his plate with the glazed, succulent meat.

Chapter 35

"Okay, Kate's all settled in the beanbag with a pile of bug books. She's happy as a clam. So let's get started." Emma carefully threaded the end of the film into the old microfiche reader. "It's hard to believe we still use such old technology." The movement felt clumsy and awkward compared to the touch-screen computer she was used to at the circulation desk.

"'Old' is relative, I suppose." Jake pulled a chair close to Emma and peered over her shoulder.

The microfiche equipment was tucked away in an upstairs room of the library—a room that was rarely used and contained the dust of several decades. The machine stood on a scarred wooden table and was flanked on either side by files filled with film.

"All of that history stored in a couple of metal cabinets," said Emma as she began to scroll down the page. "Hmmm, let's see. Should we start around 1984?"

"Probably 1985." Jake leaned in closer and Emma could smell the faint scent of soap on his skin. She felt her heart flutter and was annoyed. Now was not the time to notice such details!

"It must be strange for you ... I mean it was your wife's mother." Emma spoke suddenly, hoping to break the spell of Jake's nearness and stared out the small, lace-covered window across the main street of the little town. He followed her gaze and saw bookstore owner Laurence George and Nanette walking toward the Spare Change Diner. The church chimes rang the quarter hour. The ancient oak trees swayed in the morning breeze, and a blackbird took off from one of the highest branches. "Strange to think my own mother-in-law walked these same sidewalks decades ago. What was it that William Faulkner said?" he murmured. "'The past is never dead. It's not even the past.'"

"I love Faulkner. I didn't know you were a lover of literature!"

"Back in Boston when I was a kid, I went to the library every Saturday and checked out at least two books. It was a huge library. I loved to read. Still do." Jake's gaze was far away, remembering.

"Are you sorry you moved here?" The minute the question left her mouth, Emma regretted asking it. Her face flushed pink. He'd think she was fishing for a compliment.

Jake smiled and resumed his position hovering over her shoulder.

"No, Emma. Kate and I needed to put down roots. I couldn't think of a better place for us to settle than here in Custer's Mill, where Mirabelle grew up. I had hoped if we moved into Ruth's old house, the house where Mirabelle was raised, that Kate would be able to feel closer to her mother. Of course, nothing is ever simple, is it?"

Emma shook her head and continued to scroll through the old issues of the *Custer's Mill Star*. Although she was on a specific mission, she found that she was barely paying attention to the headlines. Why did life have to be so complex? Suddenly Jake yelled, "Stop!" Emma jumped and halted her scrolling.

"Sorry, didn't mean to scare you. But look at this page. July 4, 1985. I think it's the July Fourth celebration. You know, the day of the fire."

The center snapshot showed Main Street with rows of flags on both sides of the street. The gazebo in the town center was draped in patriotic bunting. Townspeople were standing around waving flags. They all looked so festive, with no inkling of the tragedy that was to take place that night.

She scrolled down to the article about the fire and both she and Jake read through it in silence.

"Since the investigation was to be continued, we may need to look at papers later in the week." Emma's voice rose in excitement as the microfiche whirred past images and text, racing across the screen. "They should still be on this film . . . Here!" She stopped on the front page for July 7, 1985. They stared at the image of the old house with its walls charred and front windows broken.

"It looks pretty bad doesn't it?" said Jake softly. "Wonder if Mirabelle knew about these details. She never told me about it."

He read it aloud. "'Ms. Kathryn Porter, daughter of Ruth Porter, died late on July fourth from smoke inhalation. The fire, originally thought to be an accident, is now considered suspicious. County police have taken in several people for questioning concerning the fire and death. The fire marshal is assisting in the investigation. The names of the persons being questioned have not been released.'"

"Why wouldn't they release their names?" asked Emma.

"Well, if they were under the age of eighteen, the law protects their identity. Wait, what's this?"

Jake put his hand on top of Emma's and she stopped scrolling immediately. The headline seemed to take up the entire screen although, in reality, it wasn't any larger than the other news headings: "Steinbacher Taken into Custody for Porter Fire."

"Hiram!" they both said at once. "Hiram set the fire?"

"Looks that way," said Jake as he scanned the report.

"I can't believe it! Aunt Mia didn't say anything about it yesterday." Emma shook her head. "Hiram's eccentric but not cruel. He wouldn't hurt any living thing. Why, I've seen him take care of baby birds that have fallen from the nest."

"There's a vast difference between baby birds and humans, Emma. I've run across hardened criminals who wouldn't dream of hurting animals."

"Well Hiram is not a hardened criminal. No police accusation from the past is going to make me believe he was the one who started the fire! Billy mentioned Hiram was in jail as a young man. Guess we know why now."

Jake rubbed his chin and stared off into the distance. "I really need to check into this. I'll go back to the office and do some research."

Emma nodded. "I would imagine the police files and reports would give us more information than we can find here in the old newspapers. But I still think it's a big mistake. Hiram wouldn't burn down a house!"

"There's a lot we don't know about the man," said Jake softly. "I hope you're right." He stood up. "Ready to call it a day?"

Emma nodded. "Well," she hesitated, "there's one more thing I want to look up—articles about Kath's funeral." Emma once more scrolled through the files until she reached the front page for July ninth. A large picture showed Kath's mother, Ruth, and several people standing around the casket at the Rosemary Street Cemetery. Emma squinted and looked closer. "Why, that's my Uncle Albert in that picture! He seems to be comforting Ruth . . . do you see, Jake? He has his arm around her!" Emma sat back in her seat, her thoughts racing.

Jake leaned forward to get a better look. "He does seem to be very protective of her. What was his relationship to Ruth and her daughter?"

Emma looked at Jake stunned. "I don't know. Uncle Albert never talked about Ruth or Kath. I think I'll make a copy of this picture and ask him about it."

"While you're printing copies of this picture, I think we should make copies of the other pictures and articles we've found. I'm sure Mia would be interested in reading them, and you may want to show them all to your uncle, maybe to jar his memory." Jake pushed back his chair and stood up. "Early tomorrow morning, I'll start searching the records on the computer database. I'll let you know what I find out, since it looks like you're my deputy research assistant for family history." He grinned, then his face became serious. "But, Emma, remember. The Bertha Brubaker investigation is different than this. It's a police investigation for murder and it's not something I want you to be involved in. Okay?"

"Of course. I'll leave it to the experts." Emma looked down, her hand on the yellow spiral notebook. "But I am going to give Uncle Albert a call and see what he knows about all this."

"Before we go..." Jake hesitated and glanced around the small room. "I was wondering if you'd like to go out to dinner with me on Saturday evening? Nanette's invited Kate over to the farm, and I think you and I could both use an evening away from the drama of small town life." He grinned.

"Of course!" Emma hoped she didn't sound too eager. "I'd love to go to dinner. I'm not sure we'll escape the drama, though. It seems to float in the drinking water here in Custer's Mill."

Jake smiled at Emma. "Shall we go tear Kate away from those bug books now? We need to get home, and I have to stop by Billy's house on the way."

"Oh, really, why?"

"Never mind, my curious friend. Police business." Jake watched Emma's expression. "You're cute when you pout."

"I'm not pouting, Mr. Secret Agent. Now let's get Kate."

Jake pulled into Billy's driveway. "Stay here, Kate, I'll be right back." He set the door lock and walked to the front door. It was open. He tapped on the frame.

"Jake, nice to see you on a Sunday afternoon!" Billy's voice was jovial.

"Billy." Jake nodded.

"Come in. Make yourself comfortable."

"No thanks, Billy. This'll only take a minute. I'm here to let you know you need to come to the Mill County Police Department next Friday for questioning on the matter of your aunt's death." His voice was soft but firm.

"Questioning? But you've already done that, Jake. And I didn't murder my aunt. So is this really necessary?" Billy's eyes narrowed and his voice took on a threatening tone.

"Yes, it is. Please be there promptly at one. I'm sure you want this over with as soon as possible. So do I."

"Well, I guess I have no choice. But this better be the last time."

"That remains to be seen, Billy. I'll see you Friday."

Emma looked at the clock. Just past nine. Probably not too late to give her uncle Albert a call. She really would like to have him fill in some gaps about the fire that had taken the life of Kath Porter. She'd ask him if she could stop by his house. She'd have plenty of time before her dinner date with Jake. If fact, she'd just have Jake pick her up there. Then he'd have a chance to talk to Uncle Albert as well.

151

Chapter 36

"I can't wait to see the goats again! And Miss Nanette said I could *possibly* ride the horses this time! What does possibly mean? When will we get there?" Kate bounced as she spoke, despite the restrictions of her car seat.

"Whoa, there, young lady," said Jake, laughing. "One question at a time. Possibly means maybe. And we'll be there in a few minutes. Did you know Miss Nanette also has alpacas? That's where she gets the yarn she knits with."

"Wait a minute. You mean she knits with animals? How does that work?"

"No, silly! She uses their wool. Every year she has someone come to the farm and they shear the alpacas – cut their wool off. She washes the wool and spins it into yarn."

"In-ter-est-ing." Kate drew the word out as she gazed at her dad, eyebrows raised in question.

" Don't roll your eyes at me, pumpkin! It's true! Alpacas are like llamas—you know, from Peru. Some people raise them around here because they like the wool they can gather and make into yarn, like the yarn you used. Just ask Miss Nanette."

Kate's face lit up as they pulled into Nanette's long, winding lane.

Nanette held a white plastic pail in her hands and her jeans were covered with mud. Or at least, Jake hoped it was mud.

"Well, there you are, youngin'" she said, as Kate unfastened her seatbelt and hopped out of the car..

"Now, then," said Nanette, "Let me wash my hands and we'll go inside for a few minutes. Then you can help me feed the chickens. Jake, you coming?"

"I'd love to, Nanette, but I'm supposed to be at Mia's right now. We have a meeting at Professor Nelson's house in about ten minutes."

"Well, off with you, then," said Nanette. "Kate and I have work to do. See ya later!"

"Bye dad." Kate waved and blew Jake a kiss.

Jake's heart twisted as he waved. He breathed a prayer. "God, please keep her safe. Don't let anything happen to my sweet Kate." He turned the car around and headed back toward town. He turned onto Mia's street, and glanced into his rearview mirror.

The same gray Chevette that had been following him since he left Nanette's farm continued to tail him. Coincidence? Probably. Still, he took note of the license tag. Maybe he'd look it up when he got back to the office.

Mia was at the door ready to go as soon as Jake knocked.

Though it was early evening, the temperature was still nudging the nineties. The sun was low in the sky. Jake adjusted his sunglasses to ward off the strong glare that was peeking in around the edges of the plastic frames and tugged at his shirt collar as if he wanted to rip it from his neck.

Jake was grateful to finally reach the professor's house.

"Come in and cool off!" Emma held the door open and the two entered the cool, dark foyer of the old house. "I've made some lemonade," Emma called over her shoulder as they walked down the long hall toward the center room that her great-uncle used as a library and a study. Although Emma's voice was polite, it was also cool. Something was definitely bothering her, Jake thought.

They found Professor Nelson sitting at his desk surrounded by the small pile of newspaper clippings that Emma had copied.

"Welcome, Jake." Professor Nelson nodded toward his guests. "Has our temperature reached the three-digit mark today?"

Jake pushed a lock of damp hair away from his forehead and nodded. "Awfully close, sir. Awfully close."

Emma poured lemonade into four crystal goblets. The sound of the ice clinking against the glass was inviting.

The professor adjusted the spectacles on his nose and cleared his throat. "Yes, the only thing hotter than the weather is the gossip in this town."

Professor Nelson shifted in his seat and cleared his throat again. He was uncomfortable and Jake was certain that his unease had nothing to do with the heat.

Emma sat on the edge of her chair and glanced quickly at her great-uncle. "Well?" She raised her eyebrows in question.

"You start," said Professor Nelson quietly.

Emma took a deep breath and looked out the bay window, almost as if in a trance. "I guess the way to start is just to jump in with both feet. Remember the picture we found in the library? The one with Uncle Albert and Ruth? Well, we were right, Jake. That picture has a lot of meaning. It seems my uncle has lived a large, important part of his life in secret."

Professor Nelson passed a veined hand over his face in a weary gesture. "I am afraid that I have disappointed my great-niece." Emma stared straight ahead and the professor continued, "I have tried to make my family proud of me, and over the years, I think I have accomplished some worthy deeds. But the most important deed of all, I have kept a secret and secrets have a way of getting out, even if it's years later when they finally come to light.

"When Emma brought that newspaper picture to show me, I was flooded with memories. I can feel the hurt and anger as if it were yesterday." The professor's eyes began to tear up and he took a minute to compose himself. "You see, Kath was my daughter. Mine and Ruth's." He paused briefly as if expecting a reaction. When they were silent, he continued, "Ruth and I had been in love as long as I can remember. We grew up here together in Custer's Mill. I never loved another woman. Of course, back in those days it was socially unacceptable for a white man to marry a black woman. Silly laws! The human heart cares nothing about the pigment of one's skin." The tears spilled, flowing down his chin and into his beard.

Emma handed him a tissue and reached to take hold of his other hand. "My uncle and Ruth were married in secret. His deep love for Ruth was real. They did the best they could at a time when mixed marriages were difficult, if not nearly impossible. He kept it a secret so that his family would not be hurt by his actions. Or try to stop the marriage."

"I guess you realize," said the professor, turning to Jake, "that my news impacts you and Kate more than most. Yes, I am Mirabelle's grandfather—Kate's great-grandfather."

Jake sat stone still, staring intently at the elderly man. Professor Nelson continued, "Ruth and I mutually agreed that secrecy would be the best thing. We worked it out that she would stay in her home place, and that I would go on to complete my education at the College of William and Mary. The years just seemed to roll along. By the time Kath was born, I was a full professor and Ruth was quite settled in her own life. We lived our lives separately, but were as close as we could be, without giving ourselves away."

There was a deepening silence in the room. Somewhere a fly buzzed and outside, the trill of a sparrow filled the air. Finally Mia spoke. "So that's why you were in the picture. That's why you had your arm around Ruth. It all makes sense now."

"Does it? Does it really?" A note of bitterness had crept into the professor's voice. "I'm afraid what would have made the most sense was for me to publicly acknowledge Ruth as my wife and Kath as my daughter." His voice trailed off and his face filled with pain.

Emma put her arm around her great-uncle. "Uncle Albert, they need to know the rest of the story. Please. Especially Jake."

The professor sighed. "Yes, well, you see, Ruth was only part African American. Her father was William Brubaker Senior. His wife died when Bertha was born. Ruth's mother, Elsie, went to the mansion to help take care of the newborn infant and her older brother, William Junior. Eventually, William Senior and Ruth's mother became romantically involved. As far as I know, only Ruth knew the truth about her father and her ancestry. Ruth and Bertha grew up together in the same house and became best friends. Old man Brubaker adored those girls. They were only two years apart. According to the stories Ruth told me, he doted on Ruth just as much as he did on Bertha.

"On Bertha's sixteenth birthday, he gave them both identical compass rose necklaces. The compass rose is the Brubaker family's symbol. You may have seen the large quilt hanging in Bertha's parlor. Ruth cherished her necklace but never wore it in public. She gave it to Kath when she turned sixteen. It was one of the few things they found unharmed after the fire. Her death was especially tragic, because Ruth was always so cautious with Kath. Why, she wouldn't even let the local boys like Billy or Pete come near her daughter."

Emma drew in her breath sharply. "The necklace! I saw that necklace on Kate the day I met her at the library. Is that Ruth's necklace?"

Jake nodded. "I guess it must be. It was one of the pieces I found in Mirabelle's jewelry box after the accident. Kate fell in love with it, and I let her wear it. Thought it might help her feel closer to her mother."

"Uncle Albert, you didn't tell me about the compass rose necklace! I think I found Bertha's in her day planner! Does that mean that Kath would have been in line to inherit some of the Brubaker fortune if she had lived?"

Professor Nelson scratched his head. "Well, William Brubaker didn't put anything in his will that named Ruth or Kath as a beneficiary. Not that I know of. He did make sure that a small trust was in place for Ruth and her descendants. Those funds helped to rebuild the house after the fire."

"Maybe that's what Bertha was looking for in the library vault." Emma moved to the edge of her seat. "Proof of Ruth's heritage and her connection to the Brubaker family. Maybe she was going to bring this information to light and change her will."

Professor Nelson rose unsteadily to his feet. "You all must remember that we have to keep this information to ourselves for now. Any one of us with this knowledge might be in danger."

Chapter 37

Billy drove down Rosemary Street and slowed to gaze at the elegant Brubaker mansion. He had big plans for the place once legal matters had been settled with his Aunt Bertha's estate. He might open up a bed and breakfast—or even a hotel. Once the new highway was built, Custer's Mill would become a desirable destination for tourists. They would bring their big-city dollars and come to breathe the fresh country air, hike in the national forest, and exclaim over the beautiful mountain vistas. Yes, he thought, no matter what, he could make this work. He'd make something of himself after all.

Too bad his dad wouldn't be here to see it. He always said Billy would never amount to anything.

But today, he needed to find the papers Aunt Bertha showed him the day she died. Where were they?

As he stepped out of his car, he glimpsed two figures approaching the rose garden. Trespassers were not welcome on his property, or the soon-to-be-his property, that is. He left the door ajar so he could catch the miscreants unaware. He hoped they hadn't heard him approach.

He made his way up the stone pathway through the roses and peered around the corner of the guest cottage. Aha! It was two of those old biddies, those busybody friends of his aunt, Jane Allman and Marguerite White. They had no right to be here!

"Ladies! Miss White! Mrs. Allman!" Billy yelled, causing the two women to jump and step backward from the rose bushes they were inspecting.

"Good grief, Billy, you scared us to death," said Jane. "No need to yell. We're just clipping a few of your aunt's favorite roses to put on her grave. I'm sure you don't mind."

"Well," Billy's voice was harsh, "matter of fact, I do mind. I don't want folks thinking they can just come out here any time they want. It *is* private property, you know."

The women glanced at each other, eyebrows raised. Marguerite whispered to Jane, "Reminds me of an angry rooster with that red cap and all his flapping and crowing." They both giggled.

Billy chose to ignore their amusement. "Aunt Bertha's gone. I don't expect her friends to be coming around here without my permission." He placed his hands on his hips and glared at the women.

Marguerite's expression changed to cool disdain. "We do beg your pardon, sir, if you consider gathering roses for your aunt's grave to be trespassing. Perhaps we should just leave."

"Billy, we're almost done," Jane's voice was soft and soothing. "We'd appreciate you allowing us to finish up before we go."

"Well, go ahead," said Billy. "But make sure you ask me first if you want to come back here for any reason."

The women looked at each other again and shrugged, then began to snip several long stems of fragrant red and yellow roses. They placed them in a bucket of water.

"On our way out, let's see if there are any peach roses left," said Jane, as they picked up the bucket and headed toward the lane. "Bertha loved those roses."

They turned down a narrow pathway in the garden and looked back at Billy, who was watching them from the top of the garden, his hands still on his hips.

"What's that?" asked Marguerite, pointing to a glimpse of red and blue along the path. As they approached the spot, Jane bent down. "It's an old glove." Suddenly, she let out a scream.

"Billy, come quickly! It's Hiram!"

Billy ran down the path to where the ladies were standing, hands over their mouths, their eyes wide with shock.

"What is it?" he asked, out of breath.

The glove in the pathway was attached to the hand of Hiram Steinbacher, who was lying on his side, mostly hidden by the thick foliage at base of the peach rose bush.

"Is he . . ." stammered Jane. "Is he dead?"

"Hey, you," Billy said, his voice cracking slightly with fear. A strong odor of alcohol wafted up in the warm air. "Are you drunk? Wake up! You're just like your old man after all. You loser."

Billy prodded him with the toe of his shoe, rolling Hiram's inert body onto its back. Hiram's right arm, which had covered his face, flopped down onto the moist grass.

"See if he has a pulse, Billy. Quickly. We need to call an ambulance." Marguerite knelt down beside the body.

Billy grimaced. There was no escaping touching Hiram's filthy, sweaty neck. He knelt down and checked for a pulse with as little contact as possible. He wiped his hand on his pants leg and looked at the two ladies peering down at him. "He's alive. He's drunk!" Billy's face took on a look of disgust. "The stinkin' drunk just passed out."

"Still," said Marguerite, "we have to call an ambulance. He might have alcohol poisoning, and we're not leaving him lying here in the rosebushes on a hot day like this. Get out your phone and call. Now."

Billy reluctantly punched in the numbers.

Jane and Marguerite stood guard over the unconscious Hiram, and had begun bathing his forehead with a white lace handkerchief rung out with water from the flower bucket. The sound of their voices drifted toward Billy, but he couldn't hear what they were saying. He didn't really care. He was tired. Tired of a lot of things. He just wanted to find those papers and go home.

At the sound of sirens, Billy sat up and arranged a concerned look on his face. You're the town manager after all, he told himself. Buck up. He was standing near the cottage when the ambulance pulled into the lane.

"This way, gentlemen." Billy gestured toward the rose garden.

After a brief assessment of Hiram's condition, the paramedics loaded him into the ambulance and whisked him away to the hospital, sirens blaring.

As the ambulance siren faded away, two more sirens approached, first Pete's squad car, then Jake in a county vehicle.

"Man, am I glad to see you." Billy shook Pete's hand with enthusiasm. "Hiram's gone on a binge after all these years and drunk himself unconscious."

"That so? What are you doing out here, anyhow?"

Billy shrugged. "Just checking on the place. Good thing, too, since a couple of my aunt's old biddy friends decided to invite themselves here to cut some roses for her grave. Trespassing."

Pete glanced up and scowled at the two women who remained in the rose garden.

"Hello Pete. Billy." Jake had walked over to Billy's car to greet the men, a grim expression on his face. "Heard the call. So what's happened? Who's hurt? And what are you doing here, Billy?"

"Well, this is my property. I have a right to be here. But those two ladies, they were trespassing." He pointed at Jane and Marguerite, still talking quietly in the rose garden.

"Sounds like Hiram went on a classic bender to me." Pete shook his head. "Shame. And I thought Hiram gave that up a long time ago. But you never know what drives some folks, right, Jake? We see that all the time in our line of work." He winked at Jake.

"Pete I need you to keep people off this property. We have a murder investigation going on."

Pete gave Jake a curious look. "You have any news on that front, buddy?"

"Until I finish my investigation, this place is off-limits for everyone. No exceptions. That's your job, Anderson. Keep everybody off this property."

"I'm on it, Detective." Pete saluted and headed down the lane to disperse the growing crowd of curiosity-seekers. Billy's car was already gone.

Jake hailed Marguerite and Jane. After they had answered his questions about events surrounding their discovery of Hiram, he sent them on their way, warning to stay off the property. He stood, arms crossed, and looked around the garden, as if willing it to speak and give him a clue. Instinct told him Hiram's drinking binge was connected to Miss Brubaker's death. But how?

A glint of light inside the rosebush caught his attention. He reached in and pulled out an empty whiskey bottle, trying to avoid nasty snags on his skin or his shirt. Petals and water rained down on the ground, stirring up a heady scent.

The bottle was empty. One sniff told him it was whiskey, all right, but he'd take it to the lab for testing, just to be sure.

Maybe Hiram had indeed fallen off the wagon and drunk himself into a stupor.

Jake intended to find out.

Chapter 38

"There ain't no two ways about it; young Billy Brubaker is gonna be a rich man." Reba dropped two sugar cubes into her cup of black coffee, stirred the mixture and dropped in two more. "Why I bet that house alone is worth a million or more . . . and then there's the land."

Nanette stabbed at her sunny-side-up eggs. "True. I could understand Billy wanting Bertha out of the way. Far as I know, there's nobody else to get that money but him."

"It does make a person suspect that Bertha was murdered," Jane leaned in and lowered her voice. "But she was old. You'd think that if it was Billy that did her in, he could have waited a couple more years until she died a natural death."

"There's something awfully strange in all of this and now old Hiram's fallen off the wagon after all these years." Nanette soaked some of the runny yellow egg into her toast. "What do you think, Marguerite? You've been awfully quiet over there."

Marguerite adjusted the silver-rimmed spectacles on her nose, cleared her throat, and began. "I've been doing a lot of thinking lately. This whole thing seems a bit beyond belief. First they want to build a road through our town, then Bertha dies from poison. We've had an attempted kidnapping, and now, there's Hiram. Makes you wonder if there's a connection. I wonder if Bertha knew something that somebody didn't want the rest of us to find out."

"That's pretty far-fetched," said Nanette. "I personally think Bertha's death was accidental. She might've died of one of those herbal concoctions she was always talking about—got some belladonna into it by mistake."

"We may never know," said Marguerite.

It was just past noon when Marguerite heard the sharp rap of the doorknocker. She looked up from the spreadsheet on her computer and sighed. Just when she was so close to finishing her personal bookkeeping for the month. Maybe if she ignored the knocking, the person at the door would assume she was not at home and go away. She typed in a series of numbers and tried to concentrate on balancing her checkbook. But the persistent rapping continued. It was no use. She'd just as well deal with the interruption. Wearily, she answered the door.

"Emma!" Marguerite recovered herself in time to be civil. "What a surprise."

"I'm sorry to barge in on you like this, Marguerite, but I have something important to show you. Do you have a minute?" Emma looked past Marguerite to the kitchen table piled with bills and receipts. "Oh, I see you're busy. I'm sorry for barging in on you like this." Emma started to back away.

"I can spare a few minutes for my favorite librarian. What's up?"

Emma found a clear corner on the table and began to lay out the pages of Bertha's planner.

"Ah, what have we here?" Marguerite pulled her glasses down the bridge of her nose and peered at the pile of papers.

Emma looked slightly abashed. "These are copies from a planner that Miss Bertha accidentally left at the library. You know. Before she died."

"Well I wouldn't assume they were left *after* she passed." Marguerite smiled. "I assume you have turned the original planner over to the police?"

"Yes. But I thought I should make copies. Just in case."

"So how can I help?" Marguerite pulled a chair back to sit next to the planner copies.

"Well," began Emma, "I have been intrigued with the idea that the key to Miss Bertha's death might somehow be in that old basement vault. You know, she visited it right before – you know – right before she died. I have been trying to get into the old safe for awhile now, but I can't figure out the combination."

"Emma, are you sure this shouldn't be a job for the police?" Marguerite looked troubled.

"Maybe, but they refuse to take it seriously. Pete pretty much told me that I was a silly spy and Jake wants me to stay out of the way of the investigation. But I can't just leave it. I'm really convinced that there are clues in that vault."

"I see. And how do I fit into this picture?" asked Marguerite, glancing at the pile of work she still needed to finish.

"My eureka moment came this morning. Thank goodness I could get away at lunch and you're at home. For some reason, I remembered that you did a little code work for the CIA back in the sixties."

Marguerite nodded. "A bit. Yes."

"So I was wondering if you'd give me a crash course in interpreting codes. I think there's something in this planner that has the combination to the vault."

"A crash course in code breaking? Now that's a new one!" Marguerite laughed. "I studied six years to learn just the basics. Codes are complex communication devices."

Emma looked deflated. "So there's nothing you can tell me that can help?"

"Well, I only have a few minutes now," Marguerite said. "We can schedule a time to work on it again next week." She stressed the word *schedule* ever so slightly.

Seeing Emma's downcast face, Marguerite continued. "Show me what you have. Let's see what we're up against."

Emma brightened and handed Marguerite a page. "See this? I thought maybe it was initials, but now I'm not so sure. Do you think it might be a code?"

Marguerite looked at the series of numbers. "Quite possibly. But codes work on keys. Bertha must have stashed the key to her code somewhere. You'll need to find it. A basic code uses the alphabet and can start with different letters. A letter can represent a number and vice versa. So once you have the key to the cipher, you can count letters from there and figure out the code. It may take a bit of time, but if it's not complex, you'll be able to solve it."

"But how can I possibly find Bertha's key? We're not allowed in her house. Even if the police would let us, Billy would have a fit. Did you ever talk with Bertha about your job?"

"There were many things about my job that I could discuss with no one." Marguerite spoke slowly. "But I do remember several generic conversations with Bertha about codes and code breaking. Of course, code breaking was nothing then like it is now. Now it's computer hacking and internet breaches. Back then, we did it all by hand."

"I was thinking that if you had talked to Bertha about codes, she may have used the information you gave her to remember the vault combination. Not recently, but maybe years ago when you were both—well, younger."

"That's an interesting possibility. Let me give it some thought."

Marguerite stood up, and Emma took the cue.

"Thank you so much for your time, and for your thoughts. I'll keep working on this code. I really think that the vault could hold the key to the motive behind Bertha's murder."

Marguerite looked thoughtful. "Maybe you're on to something. Just maybe."

"By the way, Marguerite, I would be grateful if you kept this code stuff to yourself. I don't really want the other library volunteers jumping on the idea. I need some time to process it on my own."

"Of course. Codes are meant to be kept secret." Marguerite winked and Emma smiled.

"Thanks again. I may be running down a wrong path on this whole idea, but I'd like to see it through until I hit a definite roadblock."

Marguerite sat down at her table and stared at the screen saver on her computer, a seed of an idea growing in her mind.

Chapter 39

Jake was within two blocks of Valley Hospital when he pulled his cruiser into the left lane, preparing to make the turn. Hiram wouldn't be able to tell him much. Pete said Hiram was still in a coma. No real change from when the paramedics brought him in.

Jake needed to see for himself, though. Sometimes the local grapevine was less than accurate. Alcohol poisoning was the preliminary diagnosis. Trouble was, nobody in town ever saw Hiram drink. There was also something fishy about the bottle being hidden in the bushes. For some reason, it was difficult for Jake to imagine Hiram drinking himself into a stupor and then taking time to hide the bottle. He was glad he'd sent it off for testing.

The volunteer at the reception desk directed him to Hiram's room on the second floor. The hallway was clear, and two nurses were huddled around a computer monitor. They didn't even look up when he walked by. He made a mental note about the lack of security, partly out of habit.

The door to 205 was propped open and he could see Hiram under the sheets, pale and as still as a corpse. Jake cleared his throat and spoke in a clear, slow voice. "Mr. Steinbacher, can you hear me?" The figure on the bed did not respond. "Mr. Steinbacher, I would like to talk about what happened to you." Jake stood there feeling foolish. It was obvious that Hiram didn't hear a word.

"What are you doing here, Detective Preston?" Jake looked up. Hiram's daughter, Sissy, brushed past him and stood by her father's side. She looked tired and drawn.

"Hello, Mrs. Lambert. How are you?" Jake pulled out a chair and motioned for the young woman to sit down.

Sissy shook her head. "No, I need to stand here in case he wakes up." Sissy brushed a few grey strands from her father's weathered forehead.

Jake nodded. "Of course. I just came to see how your father was doing. I thought maybe he might be able to talk and shed some light on what happened to him."

Sissy's face brightened a bit and she gave him a slight smile. "You mean you don't think he drank himself into a coma? You think something else happened to him?"

Jake moved to the other side of the bed so he faced Hiram's daughter. "Right now, I don't know what to think. What have the doctors said?" His voice was gentle and Sissy seemed to relax.

"Well, the doctors told me he smelled of liquor when they found him. His blood alcohol level was .35. That was sure high enough to put him in a coma. In fact, doc said that he's lucky he isn't dead." Sissy held on to the metal rail of the bed as though needing the extra support. "They still don't know for sure, though. They're going to run some more tests. But I don't think for a minute my daddy did this to himself."

A groan came from the bed, and Sissy reached for her father's hand.

"Daddy, can you hear me? It's Sissy. Wake up now!" Sissy's voice was pleading, but Hiram had stilled. She pulled the covers up around him and ran her hand over his brow. "You just rest then. You're still so tired."

Jake looked at the young woman bent over the hospital bed. She looked as though she could use a long rest as well.

"I know for a fact, my daddy hasn't had a thing to drink in over twenty years," Sissy continued. "He saw too much of that with his own father, and he didn't want to be like him." She shook her head. "I just don't know what happened. Some folks think he's weird, but I know he is a good and honest man." Sissy took out a handkerchief from her pocket and dabbed at her eyes. "People are saying you're a good man too, Detective Preston, and I can see that about you. Please find out what really happened, because it sure can't be what that paramedic reported. My daddy doesn't drink!"

Hiram began to stir again. His lips moved and his eyelids fluttered. Sissy grabbed her father's hand again. "Daddy, wake up. Come back to us. Detective Preston, I've got to go get the doctor. Please stand here with him a minute in case he wakes up or says something." Sissy ran from the room.

Jake looked down at the frail man. Instinctively he reached out to place his hand on Hiram's arm. Suddenly, Hiram's eyes opened and for a minute the two men stared at each other. Then Hiram spoke. The words came out in a hoarse whisper, but Jake had no trouble understanding what the older man was saying. "Be sober and self-controlled. Be watchful," Hiram rasped. "Your adversary the devil walks around like a roaring lion, seeking whom he may devour." With a sigh, as though this effort had exhausted him, Hiram closed his eyes and once again lost consciousness.

Jake felt a chill over his whole body. Was Hiram was trying to warn him—or at least make him aware of something . . . but what? Or was this just another rant?

Sissy returned with a young doctor who glanced at Jake, nodded a greeting and asked them both to step out into the hallway while he examined the patient. Jake didn't mention Hiram's cryptic message. He was still trying to process the whole eerie scene.

Jake led Sissy to the waiting room. He had to get her to sit down, if just for a moment. The poor woman looked ready to keel over. He filled a cup with water from the water cooler and handed it to her. She looked up at him, gratefully.

"Detective Preston, I don't have anyone else to help me. I sure won't go to that Pete Anderson. He's hated my daddy ever since they were young. My daddy went to jail for something he didn't do. He suffered for some other person's sin. Miss Brubaker helped get him out on parole. I think they knew he was innocent. Anyway, my daddy has been trying ever since to get people to believe in him." Sissy hung her head. "He's a good man. I don't think a lot of people understand him, but he has a heart of gold. He loved Miss Brubaker. She trusted him when others didn't. He would've done anything for her."

Jake took the empty cup from her and tossed it into the trash can. "Mrs. Lambert, I assure you that I'll make every effort to find out

168

what happened to your father. Can you think of anything else that might help me understand this whole situation?"

Sissy looked at Jake with a hint of hope and trust in her eyes. "Well, I've been cleaning up his old green Chevy van while he's been in the hospital. Here. I found this picture lying on the seat. I think it might be evidence." She reached into her pocket and handed Jake an old dog-eared photo.

"Evidence?" Jake raised his eyebrows slightly.

"Why, yes. He thought that Miss Brubaker was murdered, and I think someone tried to get rid of him for what he suspected."

Jake held the photo up to the light. Four grinning teenagers beamed up at him from the old snapshot. "That girl looks like the photos I've seen of Kath Porter. Am I right?"

"Yes sir, and Billy Brubaker, Shep Crawford, and the police chief himself, Pete Anderson. Daddy said they were all friends. Thick as weeds, he said."

Jake tilted the photo and squinted. "Well I'll be ..." he whispered under his breath. Kath was wearing the compass rose necklace. Jake turned to Sissy. "So, Mrs. Lambert, what did your father tell you about this picture?"

"No, it's not so much about the photo, because I really hadn't seen it before. But he told me once that those boys were trouble, especially in their younger days. There was no love lost between them and my daddy, that's for sure. He said Kath's momma, Ruth, didn't like them all hanging around and finally made Kath stop seeing them."

Jake shook his head. "Yes, I've heard she didn't like those guys near Kath. Thank you for showing me the picture, but I really don't know how this can be evidence."

"Just turn it over Detective Preston, and look what's on the back!"

Jake turned over the picture and saw in large bold print: *MURDERER!* He glanced quickly at Hiram's daughter. "Murderer? Which one do you think he was talking about?"

Sissy shook her head. "Well, I think my daddy knew secrets about things, and he felt there was a murderer among them. I think that picture is enough to bring suspicion on them for something."

"That could be, Mrs. Lambert, but I'll need to check into this before I can speculate. I'm not sure what it means, but I'll keep this picture and see if I can find out any more information."

"I'm grateful to you, Detective Preston. And I'm thankful for you taking an interest in my daddy. I'd better get back in the room and see what the doctor has to say."

Jake watched Sissy walk across the hall into Hiram's room. He held the picture and looked again at the smiling faces. Suddenly, he had an idea. So far, he had not been successful searching for files in the juvenile records that matched the date of the fire. But what if he searched by a name? Jake put the picture in his jacket pocket and walked toward the elevator door.

Hiram's words played again in Jake's mind as he stepped into the elevator: "Be sober and self-controlled. Be watchful. Your adversary the devil walks around like a roaring lion, seeking whom he may devour."

Chapter 40

Jake stretched his arms above his head to relieve some of the stiffness in his neck and back. After returning from the hospital, he had worked steadily for about an hour, reading the juvenile investigation report on William Brubaker III. The information focused on Billy's connection to the fire that had taken Kath's life. Billy had confessed to being near the Porter house earlier in the day. He said he was at the Fourth of July festival in the evening. One of Billy's witnesses was Ruth Porter. Ruth said she remembered seeing Billy with his friends at the celebration. The fire department log placed the emergency call to the Porter house at 9:05 p.m.

Jake looked at his watch: 4:45 p.m. It was getting late, and he needed to pick up Kate from the library. The library ladies had been so kind since the incident at the park. Today, they were teaching her how to shelve books. Balancing his job as detective and being a single parent was challenging. He was grateful he had new friends to help him with Kate.

He picked up the picture Sissy had given him. If he didn't know better, he would say it was Mirabelle in that picture instead of Kath. Jake felt a pang of remorse for the loss of them both. Two young lives both ended so abruptly.

He thought of Ruth again, and how she must have mourned the loss of her daughter. Both Sissy and the professor had commented that Ruth was protective, and didn't like Billy and Pete hanging around Kath.

An embryo of an idea began to form in his mind.

He started a new search, this time for Shep Crawford, the third boy in the photograph. Once again, a juvenile record appeared on the screen. But the Fourth of July fire wasn't the only incident on Shep's record. Jake scanned the report. The police report stated that Shep had been questioned in connection with a barn fire in May of 1984, and also a fire that destroyed an outbuilding on a neighbor's farm. In both incidents, he was questioned and then released to his grandmother, Bessie.

Jake had one more thing to check. If both Billy and Shep were in the database, he wondered . . . He typed in Pete Anderson's name. The search was still loading when Pete's smiling face peeked around the door. "Impeccable timing, as usual, Chief Anderson," Jake mumbled under his breath. He moved the cursor and clicked the red *x*. This part of his investigation would have to wait.

"Jake! Are you still here? Why I thought you'd be gone by now." Pete sauntered into Jake's office without waiting for an invitation and threw his hat onto the desk.

Jake minimized the screen and tidied a pile of paper clips. "It's time for me to head out. I need to go pick up Kate and let those good ladies get back to their library duties. What brings you by my office?"

"Just in the neighborhood. Thought I'd drop in on my way back to Custer's Mill and let you know that Dove is helping me on the case. He's checking on the whereabouts of all the known perps in the area. We'll know something soon."

Jake nodded his approval and glanced toward the door. Pete took the cue.

"Well, see you later, pal!"

The two men gave each other a brief nod.

Watching until Pete pulled his cruiser away from the curb, Jake sat down to resume his search. It took a few seconds for the official record to pop up on the screen. But unlike Billy and Shep's records, Jake saw emblazoned across the screen, "Sealed."

How did you manage that, pal? Friends in high places?

Chapter 41

Billy sat alone on a bench outside the interrogation room of the Mill County Police Department. He was hunched over, elbows on his knees.

He sighed and looked up at the old clock on the wall, ticking away the seconds.

The door opened and Jake motioned to Billy. He walked into Jake's office, sat down and crossed his arms. "Don't know why I'm here. I have a town to run, you know."

Jake smiled. "I won't keep you long. I know you have a lot on your plate. It can't be easy running this town, especially with all that's going on with the highway project."

Billy's face still registered irritation, but he sat back in his chair and seemed to relax a bit. Jake gave himself a mental pat on the back. He suspected that appealing to Billy's vanity was the only way to mollify the man.

"How's that road project coming along?" Jake opened his tablet and watched the wireless icon pulsate as it searched for an Internet connection.

"Not bad. Not bad. That Jarrod Harmon sure knows what he's doing. He's already got detailed plans. Shoot, he even has a proposed plan for a new library."

"How do you think your late Aunt Bertha would react to the new library plans?"

Billy jerked his head up. "Aunt Bertha? You know she hated the thought of that old building being torn down. Why are you bringing her up now?" And then, as if suddenly realizing that his Aunt Bertha was the reason he was in the small, bare-walled room with Jake, his face reddened.

Jake tapped the touch screen and flipped open a blank document. He really preferred the old-fashioned method of pencil and paper, but the files were much easier to transfer if he compiled them electronically. "So, Billy, tell me what you know about the evening of your aunt's death."

Billy slumped in the chair again and began twirling a loose thread on his shirt sleeve. "What do you want me to say? That I killed her? That I poisoned her? If you're looking for a confession, don't look at me. I didn't have anything to do with her death. And if you're going to waste your time harassing innocent people, I'm gonna call my lawyer and have you removed from the case."

"I don't think Mr. Stewart has any jurisdiction over murder investigations," Jake said mildly. "And I don't mean to upset you, Billy. I just want to get to the bottom of this."

"And you think I don't?" Billy stood up. "I'm not taking this anymore. I've had enough." He walked toward the door.

"Sit down." Jake's voice was low, but it held a note of authority that Billy recognized. The older man sat down.

There was a light tap at the door, and Jake's sergeant entered with a folder. Jake nodded his thanks and the man left, closing the door behind him. The room was silent except for the soft tick of a clock.

"You got my records in there?" Billy moved to the edge of his chair and pointed toward the folder.

"You have a police record, Billy?"

Billy looked disgusted. "Now how do you think I got the job of town manager if I had a police record? I mean, do you have my information in that folder?"

"What kind of information might that be, Billy? You've been out of school for a long time. I doubt your cumulative records are around anymore." Jake shifted in his seat and looked at Billy directly. "Were you at your Aunt Bertha's house on the afternoon of her death?"

"Maybe. But I wasn't the last one there. Her lawyer was pulling in the driveway just as I was leaving."

"Are you suggesting that Paul Stewart had something to do with her death?"

Billy snorted. "No way. That man has been our family lawyer for decades. Why would he kill Aunt Bertha?"

"Why would anyone kill her?" Jake asked softly.

Billy stood up again. "I'm getting out of here. I don't have anything else to say to you or anybody. You're wasting my time."

"You will leave this room when I give you permission and not a minute before. Unless you'd like to become a guest in our new jail. Now sit back down. I'm not finished yet."

Billy shoved his chair against the table. "I will not sit down. You have no right to hold me here!"

"Billy, if you don't sit back down I will have you arrested for disorderly conduct."

"You will do no such thing. Get me my lawyer!"

"Sit down, Billy. One more question and you can go."

Billy stared at him with contempt, but he sat down.

"Now, I will ask you one more time," said Jake steadily. "Do you know of any reason anyone would want to harm your aunt?"

Billy put his face in his hands, and Jake had trouble hearing his muffled voice. "For the last time, no. I don't know why anybody would want to kill her. Just let her rest in peace."

Billy stood up. "Can I go now?"

Jake gave Billy a long, thoughtful look. "Yes, Billy. You may go."

Billy walked out without a word, and let the heavy metal door slam behind him.

Jake fingered the corners of the old photo on his desk. He hadn't even had a chance to show the picture to Billy. He'd try again tomorrow. Billy was the kind of man who just might benefit from a night in jail. The single-layer mattress and flat pillow would likely give him enough motivation to cooperate. That is, if he actually knew anything about the murder.

Jake glanced at the photo again. Yes. There was something there. Something he had to uncover. He wasn't sure if there was anything that linked the picture to present events, but he had a nagging feeling in the pit of his stomach that there was a connection somewhere.

Old Hiram had tried to tell him something and now the man lay in a hospital bed drifting in and out of a coma. And then there was that odd quote from Shep's grandmother. Something about "old sins and long

175

shadows." Jake thought again of William Faulkner and his cryptic quote. The air teemed with the energy of the "sins of the fathers."

The past is never dead.

Chapter 42

Jake shifted in the slick leather chair as he waited in the large conference room. It was nice of Emma to be able to watch Kate on such short notice. Staring out of the palladium window, he could see the traffic on Main Street starting to pick up with people heading home from the long workweek.

Now that he had a moment to sit quietly, Jake realized he was very tired. Not physically tired, but mentally and emotionally drained. The past few weeks had been a roller coaster of events. Each happening in itself would have been enough to wear him out: Bertha's death, the break-in at Emma's house, and the attempted kidnapping of his daughter. And then, there was Hiram. That whole situation still puzzled him. If only he could read between the lines of the older man's speeches. If only he could interpret the biblical rants that came from Hiram's mouth. And now, this. What was he doing in the prestigious law offices of Stewart, Stewart, and Sampson?

"Sorry to keep you waiting, Mr. Preston." Jake had been so lost in his thoughts that he had not heard the door open. Paul Stewart reached out to shake Jake's hand. "Especially on a Friday evening. I'm sure you're ready to start your weekend."

The door opened wider and Billy stepped in. He was dressed in his best dark gray suit, and although the pant legs were wrinkled, Jake could tell that it was an expensive cut and had once fit Billy well. Billy's slack mouth turned into a scowl when he saw Jake.

"What's he doing here?" Billy glared at Jake.

Jake attempted a smile. After all, his meeting with Billy just a couple hours ago had been a less-than-pleasant encounter.

Paul motioned for both men to take their seats while he settled into the chair at the head of the table. "Please make yourselves comfortable. We will begin the process as soon as the others arrive."

"Others?" Billy scowled. "Who else did you invite? The butcher? The baker?" Before he could continue his childish rhyme, the door burst open.

The room erupted into a swirl of polyester dresses, chattering ladies, and scooting chairs as three venerable members of the Friends of the Library entered along with Sissy, and settled themselves around the table.

"Well if this isn't a room full of grumpy old men!" Nanette pulled out a chair beside Billy and sat down with a flourish. She had dressed for the occasion in brown slacks and a purple flowered top, forgoing her usual work boots for a pair of battered leather loafers.

Paul looked grave, but there was an unmistakable twinkle in his eyes as he watched the flutter die down to whispers. He nodded toward his secretary. "Thank you, Linda. Since everyone is here now we'll begin. Please hold all of my calls until we're finished."

Jake's mind was reeling. He remembered Professor Nelson's words of caution. Did Kate's inheritance have something to do with her near kidnapping? As far as Professor Nelson knew, though, Kate wasn't in line to inherit anything. But if that was true, why was he here?

Taking a stack of papers out of a folder, Mr. Stewart walked around the table and placed a document in front of each person. "Last Will and Testament of Bertha Brubaker" was emblazoned on the front cover. "Ladies and gentlemen, we are here to initiate the reading of Miss Bertha Brubaker's will."

Sissy gave a gasp and clutched her purse. "I don't have anything to do with Miss Brubaker so I don't know why I should be asked to come here." Her face turned red, and she perched on the edge of her chair like a bird ready to take flight.

Nanette put her hand on Sissy's arm.

"Well if it makes you feel any better, Sissy, we don't know why we're here either. Bertha was our friend in her own strange way, but I certainly didn't expect her to leave us anything. I do assume that's why we're here?" She glanced at Paul, who smiled and nodded slightly. "I mean, what would I do with her musty old jewels?"

"Nanette, be quiet!" hissed Marguerite. "Nobody in her right mind would leave you any jewels. You'd just put them on the pigs' ears."

"You'd just flash them around on your fingers and end up getting robbed!" Nanette plopped her elbows on top of her copy of Bertha's will.

"Ladies, I can understand your confusion and trepidation," Paul smiled. "I assure you this mystery will all be made clear within the next few minutes." The attorney slowly unfolded the paper in front of him and directed them all to turn to the first page of their document.

Billy broke the silence. "Well, I don't understand why all of these people are here either. This is a family matter, Stewart, not a public spectacle. I should be the only one here at this reading." He puffed out his chest with an air of indignation.

Paul Stewart looked at Billy over the top of his spectacles. "Billy, you were Miss Bertha's only known living relative until recently. New documents named Ruth Porter as a legal heir of William Brubaker, your great-grandfather. Your aunt shared these documents and information with you on the day before she died. I know this, because she told me so when I visited with her that afternoon."

"Ruth Porter?" Nanette burst out. "What does Ruth Porter have to do with Bertha Brubaker? This is beginning to sound like a soap opera."

Billy narrowed his eyes and leaned forward in his chair. "Paul this is absurd. Aunt Bertha certainly did not tell me any such thing. If she had such documentation, I want you to show me the papers." Billy sat back in triumph, his arms crossed.

"That won't be necessary, Billy, as your aunt had me draw up and execute a new will prior to her death. That is what I'll be reading. Kindly refrain from any further outbursts until I am finished." Paul Stewart turned toward Jake. "Mr. Preston, you are here as guardian of Kathryn Porter Preston, great-granddaughter of Ruth Porter, her only living heir. Kate now becomes the recipient of Ms. Porter's portion of the Brubaker estate."

Jake passed a hand over his forehead. What did this mean?

Next Stewart turned to Sissy. "Mrs. Lambert, since your father is in the hospital and unable to attend this reading, I have appointed you as his representative. Miss Brubaker was insistent that Hiram be given compensation and recognition for his years of service and devotion. The rest of you need to be here because you are mentioned in the will. Now, with all of that settled. I am ready to proceed."

Everyone sat in stunned silence. Paul Stewart had their full attention. Billy looked pale.

Adjusting his glasses, the attorney began to read. "'I, Bertha Louise Brubaker, of Mill County, Virginia, being of sound mind do declare this to be my last will and testament revoking all previous wills and codicils made by me.'"

Billy snickered. "Sound mind, now that's a joke. Anyone around here knew the old girl was starting to slip."

"Kindly refrain from commenting, Billy. Not only is it annoying, but it is disrespectful." Billy was obviously pushing the limits of Paul's patience. "I will continue . . . 'I direct my executor, Paul Stewart, to pay as soon as practical after my death, all my legally enforceable debts and the costs of the administration of my estate. I give and bequeath my home and grounds to my dear friends: Jane Allman, Marguerite White, and Nanette Steele, with one stipulation: that Hiram Steinbacher be allowed to live in the garden cottage and remain employed as the caretaker of the grounds as long as he is able. Finally, I give, devise, and bequeath all the rest of my assets, real and personal, in equal interests to my living heirs, Kathryn Porter Preston and William Charles Brubaker III.'"

Billy jumped to his feet. "Why, this is an outrage! I am the only Brubaker heir, and that is that!" Billy stood there trembling. Beads of sweat formed on his forehead.

Jake sat in silence. He could only think of Kate. This had to be the reason someone tried to take her that day in the park. A chill ran down his spine to think of what could have happened. He wondered how this would change their lives. Jake thought of his beautiful little girl, happy with her new life and the friends she had made in Custer's Mill. Would he always have to be afraid for Kate's safety? Did this sad excuse for a town manager have something to do with it?

"Billy, sit down." Paul's tone was severe. "I assure you this will is official, and I intend to file it at the courthouse as soon as we finish here."

Billy stepped closer to the lawyer. "Well, I tell you this, Paul Stewart. Before I accept any of this nonsense, I want some proof. I wanna see the documents that show without a doubt that Kate Preston has a right to this money. I will contest this will, Stewart, you can bet on that." Billy raised his fist as though he were ready to take a swing at the lawyer. Then, remembering himself, he took a step back and stomped out of the room, banging the door behind him.

Chapter 43

Emma chewed on the tip of her pencil and gazed at the papers spread out in front of her. Her mind was moving in slow gear this morning. Marguerite and two new volunteers had taken the Saturday shift at the library this weekend. Emma was grateful for extra time to catch up on her sleep in Aunt Mia's lovely guest room. A bowl of sweet flakes was turning to mush and her coffee was cold.

"It's no use," she said to the ginger cat that had jumped up on the chair beside her. "I just can't concentrate." She stood and stretched, then carried her breakfast dishes downstairs to the sink. As she dumped both the cereal and the coffee into the dark tunnel of the garbage disposal, the cat meowed and looked in the direction of the cat food container. "Okay, Molasses, I'll feed you a second breakfast if you promise to let me work in peace for the rest of the morning. But only because you've behaved so well during our stay here at Aunt Mia's."

She dumped a cup of dry cat food into a plastic bowl and filled the adjoining dish with fresh water. "There. Be happy and keep quiet!" The cat crunched noisily.

Emma looked at the clock. Eight thirty. Aunt Mia had left a half hour ago to visit her brother at the farm. Thanks to Nanette Steele, Emma had been awake for two and a half hours now. Nanette had called her at six o'clock with the news that she, along with two other Friends of the Library, had inherited the Brubaker mansion! Still groggy from a deep sleep, Emma felt as though she had caught about every third word of Nanette's excited chatter. But if she had heard correctly, the ladies were now proud owners of the fanciest house in town. What would they do with their inheritance? It remained to be seen.

She needed to think. She returned to the guest room and sat down at the maple desk. As she flipped through the papers in her red folder, she paused to examine every page with notations in Bertha's neat handwriting. Along the margins for the page of March seventh, Emma noticed something she hadn't seen before: In very small, precise script, Bertha had written *B*, then *AH*. Could this be the key Emma was looking for? She jotted down the letters, and then flipped back to the beginning, scanning closely. In the margins of January third, she discovered a *BF*, then *CC*. Were these initials of someone important? She searched the rest of the pages, but found no other notations.

Emma thought back over her conversation with Marguerite. She flipped back to the numbers on May first: 12-13-37. If 12 represented the year 2012, then 13 might mean January 3 and 37 might mean March 7, the dates where the initials were written.

Emma's mind was jolted wide awake, and her skin tingled. What if the letters represented numbers? Using a simple key of A equals 1, B equals 2, and so on, then *AH* would equal 18. She quickly jotted down the rest of her solution.

Now to figure out what direction to turn the tumbler. She sat deep in thought for several minutes. Emma sat up straight. Wait a minute... The letters in March appeared in the left margin and the letters in January appeared in the right margin. The combination might be L2, then R26, then L18 then R33. It made sense, and it was a simple cipher, one Bertha could have worked out on her own.

Emma's heart pounded. She couldn't wait until this afternoon when she'd have a chance to try her solution without prying eyes around. "I've solved the cipher, Molasses! I've solved the cipher! God bless Marguerite White!" Emma picked up the cat and danced around the bedroom singing, "L2, R26, L18, R33." The cat meowed and began to purr.

Chapter 44

Emma stared at the clock, as if the intensity of her gaze would make the hands move faster. She couldn't wait to go to the vault to try the combination, but the library didn't close until three. She didn't want to answer questions about her trip to the basement, especially from the library volunteers.

The more she looked at the numbers she had deciphered, the more confident she became. She felt a surge of appreciation for Marguerite and her knowledge. In fact, her library volunteers were turning out to be a treasure trove of information and expertise. Who knew what these women would do with their new mansion and rose garden? The possibilities were intriguing.

At three thirty, Emma could stand it no longer. Surely everyone had cleared out of the library by now. She tucked the red folder into her bag, grabbed her keys, and headed out the door. This was it. Her daring adventure. She was seizing the day.

She groaned as she noticed her gas gauge had dipped past the empty mark. Although the library was nearby, she didn't want to risk running out of gas. Not today. She turned her car north in the direction of Ed's Service Station.

As she reached into her wallet for her debit card, Emma remembered too late that she had left it on the table by the computer. She felt so disorganized since she was staying with Aunt Mia. She'd been ordering books late last night and forgot to put the card back. "Great. Now I get to waste more time walking inside and paying for gas." She pushed the car door shut with a little more force than was necessary.

The interior of Ed's Service Station had not changed since Emma was a little girl. Neither, for that matter, had Ed Steiner. He always seemed to smell of gasoline and oil. His thin hair might have grayed over the years, but he'd always looked old to Emma.

Ed greeted her with his customary nod. He was never one for formalities. He just got down to the business at hand without preamble.

"Baloney and cheese, baloney and mustard, or Spam and cheese? Choose your poison, my dear." Ed rocked back on his heels and swatted at a fly buzzing around his head. "Dang flyin' bugs! Can't keep 'em out." Emma tried not to glance at the screenless open windows along the front of the building. There was not a thing blocking the flies from popping in and out of the store whenever they so pleased.

"I don't need any food today, Ed. Just ten dollars' worth of gas."

"What? No food? Just got this baloney fresh from Ted's today. Can't beat the taste of fresh baloney!"

"No thanks, Ed. I'm not much of a meat eater."

"No meat? You one of them vegetable-tarians?"

"No, I'm not a vegetarian. I'm simply not hungry at the moment. I just need gas!"

Ed gave her a look that said that he couldn't imagine anybody under any circumstance at any time not wanting baloney. He took her ten dollars and shook his head. "If you change your mind, come on back. I'll save you a chunk."

"Thanks, Ed!" Emma tried not to sound too impatient, but she could feel her excitement growing at the thought of opening the vault.

The butterflies, which had landed in her stomach earlier in the day, were turning into full-grown, fluttering luna moths by the time she inched her green Toyota into the back parking lot at the village library. The lights were off and the doors locked. She slipped her key into the lock and closed the door behind her.

Not wanting to attract unwanted attention by turning on an overhead light, Emma took a penlight from her desk drawer. That should do the trick. She pulled out the red folder and tossed her bag and phone on top of the counter. At last, she made her way to the basement.

The thin, yellow glow from the penlight made eerie shadows along the walls as Emma crept down the steps. Although she held tightly to the stair rail she knew that one false move could send her plummeting into darkness. With an involuntary shiver, she remembered the scratch marks on the vault lock. But she was being silly. If Bertha could make it down to the vault and back out again, surely she, Emma, could do the same. She hushed the nagging voice in the back of her mind, the one that reminded her that Bertha had not lived to tell about her findings.

Once in the basement, she turned on the overhead light. She would have to take that slight risk; she would need both hands and brighter illumination to try the numbers on the lock. She tucked the penlight into her pocket, took a deep breath and began to turn the rusty dial. L2, R26, L18, R33. She paused.

Every cell in her brain was focused on the lever. Even though she had felt certain of the cipher, she gasped in surprise when the bolt sprang free and the door opened. A dank, musty smell wafted out of the dark tunnel inside and Emma hesitated at the entrance.

Should she go in? Should she call Aunt Mia? Or should she call Jake?

Cautiously, she turned on her penlight and directed the narrow beam of light across the room. There were boxes stacked two deep on both sides of the doorway. One wall was lined with filing cabinets. She had no clue where to begin. In fact, she didn't even know what she was looking for.

One of the boxes looked as though it had been recently opened—the tape had been torn away and replaced loosely. Emma lifted the lid. Inside the box were labeled folders stacked in alphabetical order by title.

She picked up the first folder entitled "Birth Certificates." Emma had to look twice at the name printed on the first certificate. Yes, it said, "Ruth Porter" in clear calligraphy. In equally clear handwriting, the signature "William Charles Brubaker Sr." was first typed and then signed under the line marked "father." Her heart leapt. So it was true. Kate was in line to inherit the Brubaker fortune and here was proof positive.

Digging deeper in the box, Emma pulled out a small green ledger book and inside the front cover, in Bertha's neat handwriting, she read, "Billy's Trust Fund." Two letters were folded inside the ledger. Emma read them with growing alarm. Bertha had requested an investigation into money withdrawn from Billy's trust account. The bank's report stated that for over thirty years, Billy had been paying money into an account owned by none other than Pete Anderson.

So. Pete had been blackmailing Billy. But what for? No doubt Miss Brubaker was going to reveal this as part of her big announcement. That meant that the police chief of Custer's Mill was a murder suspect. She placed her discoveries back in the box and closed the flaps.

Leaving the vault door ajar, Emma headed up the stairs to get her phone.

"I can't wait to see Jake's face when I show him the evidence that links Pete Anderson to the murder of Bertha Brubaker."

Chapter 45

Emma punched in Mia's number and waited, drumming her fingers against her thigh in high excitement. Come on, Aunt Mia, pick up, pick up, please. But her aunt's gentle voice came only through the answering machine.

After the familiar beep, Emma spoke in a rush. "Aunt Mia, it's me, Emma. You'll never believe it! I got the library vault open and boy, are there some big surprises in there! No skeletons, though. Jake will be coming by your house soon to pick me up for our date. He'll want to see this for himself. In fact, both of you should come over here right away. Hurry!"

Emma checked the time as she returned her phone to her bag. She had to have one more look inside the vault before the others got there. She jammed her penlight into her back pocket and headed to the door leading to the basement. She stopped to listen to a faint scuffling sound. Probably just those blue jays outside the window, she thought. They'd been building a nest these last few days and generally making a racket. She started down the steps.

She had almost reached the vault when she became aware of a figure standing in the corner. A large figure. Her stomach lurched. It was Pete.

"Hello, sweetheart," said Pete. "Whatcha doing down in this dirty old cellar?" He moved toward her.

Emma's heart thumped wildly in her chest. She stepped backward and bumped into the wall next to the open vault. She took a deep breath and struggled to regain her composure.

"I should be asking you that question. What are *you* doing here?" She tried to sound authoritative and demanding.

"I think you know, Emma. I think you know."

"I know you're a wicked man, Pete."

Pete laughed mirthlessly and smiled. His voice was menacing. "I know you're a nosy little idiot, Emma. But you really don't know anything."

"Yes I do, and so do some other people."

"Oh really. And who would that be? Your new boyfriend, Jake?"

"Maybe," said Emma. "And maybe some other people. You'd better not try anything here Pete. People know."

"Sweetheart," drawled Pete, "I'm not going to try anything. It's just going to be such a shame that this old building burns down. And even sadder, when they find your bones inside."

Emma gasped, and grabbed an old broom leaning on a filing cabinet. She lunged at Pete and managed to jab him in the neck, but he knocked the broom from her hands and struck her face with his fist. The last thing she remembered was the taste of blood in her mouth as her head hit the cement floor with a smack.

Pete had already vanished when Emma awoke moments later to the acrid smell of smoke. She sat up, her head and neck throbbing with pain. She felt her mouth. Pete's blow had split her lip, but at least nothing seemed to be broken. The fall to the floor had left a huge lump on the back of her head.

Her whole body trembled as she used her feet to push herself against the wall and let it support her as she stood up. Small flames were slowly creeping from stack to stack of old newspapers and magazines, and Emma knew the entire cellar would be ablaze within minutes. Small tendrils of smoke were already getting sucked into the vault. The papers! Emma's alarm overcame her dizziness and confusion. She couldn't let them burn! Without a second thought, Emma stumbled into the vault and pulled the heavy door closed with a slam.

She stood in darkness. Emma willed herself to breathe deeply and think. Think! These papers must be saved. They were the only thing that would convict Pete of the crimes he had committed. If he succeeded, he'd not only be rid of Emma but he'd be rid of anything connecting him to Bertha's death. She pulled out the penlight and clicked it on.

Emma grabbed the incriminating papers. Clutching them in her hand, she flicked the light around. A moist, musty smell permeated the room and Emma was grateful for the thick door blocking her from the smoke. She needed to move fast. But move where? Would she soon suffocate down here? At least they'd find the papers. Unless the fire broke through the walls of the vault.

A cool draft interrupted Emma's thoughts. That was odd. Why was there a draft in here? Where was it coming from? With new resolve, she perched her penlight to shine on the wall. Ignoring her throbbing head, she shoved the shortest stack of boxes to the center of the room and was rewarded with another draft of cool air. This time the source was obvious. It came from the east wall, which was lined with three large antique oak filing cabinets.

Unable to move the first cabinet using all the strength she could muster, Emma opened the top drawer and pulled out the papers to lighten the load. Every passing second seemed like an eternity to Emma. At last she'd emptied two drawers. She put her shoulder to the old cabinet and shoved with all her might.

Slowly, it began to slide out away from the wall, and the cool draft became a gust of wind. A dark opening in the wall was framed by oak timbers. Emma worked as fast as she could to move the second filing cabinet and expose a space wide enough to squeeze past. It must be a tunnel or a cave, she thought. Did it lead outside? Was it full of water? Snakes? She shivered. But how long could she expect to survive in this vault next to a burning room full of old papers? The old building itself was a wood frame building. If it became fully aflame, the whole thing would come down.

Emma flashed a thin beam of light into the darkness and gritted her teeth. She grabbed the file of Bertha's papers, opened her shirt, and buttoned the papers inside. This ordeal would require two hands. Taking a deep breath, Emma ducked into the opening. It was just high enough for her to crawl forward on her hands and knees. The surface appeared to have a thin cement coating over the soil, but the coating had cracked away in many places and piles of crumbled, muck and slime littered the bottom of the tunnel.

She pressed forward, attempting to shine the light ahead while crawling. Not an easy feat. She chose to ignore the occasional scrabbling sounds and increasing rivulets of water. She had to focus. Focus on getting out of here alive.

And getting Pete.

Chapter 46

Jake took Mia's front steps two at a time. He was already late. He hadn't planned on staying at Nanette's farm so long. But as soon as he had stopped the car, Kate tugged him toward the barn to see the baby lambs. And then there was the long conversation with Nanette. Fortunately, she had been so excited about her plans for the Brubaker estate that she hadn't asked him about Kate's inheritance. He was still shell-shocked by the news that his daughter was about to become a rich young lady. His mind refused to process the information. The family had never lacked for anything, but they had been far from rich. Would this mean his daughter would constantly be in danger of being kidnapped and held for ransom? He tried to push these unsettling thoughts from his mind as he knocked on Mia's door.

"Hey, Jake!" Mia smiled and dusted her hands on a bright red-checked apron that already had splotches of flour down the front. "Come on into the kitchen. Would you like some cookies and coffee?"

Jake's nose detected the wonderful smell of cinnamon as he walked down the hallway into the bright, yellow kitchen. Sunlight spilled over the counter where Mia had been scooping out the dough. Two large baking sheets sat off to the side, and several dozen freshly baked oatmeal cookies were cooling in neat rows on the counter. "I'm afraid I'll spoil my dinner, but they do smell so good. Maybe just one or two!" Jake didn't wait to be asked again. He reached over and grabbed two cookies, leaving moist impressions on the waxed paper. Mia took down a blue mug from over the stove and poured Jake a cup of coffee. She placed it in front of him just as he finished the second cookie.

"Well, I guess you'll have to have another one to go with the coffee!" Mia said.

"I really shouldn't. Emma and I are going to try that new restaurant over in Haymarket. I hear they're famous for their steaks. By the way, where is Emma?" Jake looked around the kitchen, realizing he hadn't seen his dinner date since he walked in. Surely, she wasn't mad at him for being a little late!

"Oh, you're here to pick her up! Funny, I haven't seen her for some time now. I had to run to the neighbors to borrow some eggs, but that was quite a while ago. Maybe she called while I was gone." At that moment, Mia noticed the blinking red light on her answering machine in the next room. "Let me check."

Mia returned to the kitchen with a puzzled look on her face. "There was a message from Emma at 4:40 p.m. She says she got into the vault and wants us both to see what she's found."

Jake moved toward the door. "I'm heading down there. She shouldn't be going into that vault alone. Not with everything that has been happening lately."

Mia began to remove her apron. "I'm going with you."

Jake started to protest, but when he saw the determined look in Mia's eyes, he knew it was no use arguing. "Let me see if I can catch her on her cell before we head out. Maybe we're worrying for no reason." The call went through immediately, but after four rings, it switched to voice mail.

"She isn't answering. Let's go!"

The shrill blast of sirens cut through the still evening air. Jake gripped the steering wheel with both hands and willed his body to stop shaking. He swung the car into the first available parking space. Smoke poured from the basement windows of the library.

"She can't still be in there, Jake!" Mia put her hand over her mouth as a burly fireman shattered a windowpane. "We can't just sit here! We have to find her!" Mia's voice had taken on a hysterical note. Jake reached over to put a hand on her arm, but she was already out of the car and running toward the burning building.

"Ma'am," yelled one of the volunteer firefighters, "stay back! You can't go in there!" Mia started to rush past him, but he grabbed her arm. "This is a structure fire! We don't know when the walls might collapse. You can't go beyond this point!"

"But you don't understand!" Mia began to pound on the fireman's chest as though to make him see the truth. "My niece, Emma Kramer, might be in there!"

"Who?" the fireman asked sharply as he picked up his radio. "525 here," he said into the crackling box. "Could be somebody inside the building." He looked over at Mia. "Who did you say might be in there?"

"Emma! Emma Kramer! She called me from the library, but that was over an hour ago."

Jake put an arm around Mia's shoulder. "I'm Detective Jake Preston with the county police," said Jake. "We're concerned the librarian is inside. We have to send in rescue personnel immediately!"

"Detective Preston." The fireman touched his hat in acknowledgement of the officer. "We're doing all we can, sir. The guys have suited up and are going in. All we can do is sit tight and wait."

Jake felt his chest tighten. He walked through the small crowd that had gathered along the edge of the fire line, keeping an eye out for Pete. Surely he had heard the call to dispatch. Why wasn't he on the scene?

Barely pausing at the stop sign, a silver Honda Accord nosed its way past the crowd and pulled into the parking lot. Marguerite White. Jake glanced around the crowd. He suspected the other library volunteers were already here. Hopefully they would stay back and let the firemen do their job.

"Is Emma in there? Dear God, if anything's happened to her, I'll never forgive myself. Marguerite gripped Jake's sleeve as Mia walked over to join them. "I helped her with codes so she could get the combination to that vault. I'm so sorry, Mia."

Chapter 47

Emma ached all over. The muscles in her arms were throbbing and her hands and knees were caked with mud and slime. She felt like she had been climbing for miles. The narrow tunnel was toying with her claustrophobia.

After what seemed like hours, the tunnel opened to a larger passage and veered to the right. Emma moved her penlight in a circle around the walls of the cavern. Would the passage take her outside somewhere or would it just end in a solid wall of dirt and rock?

Something moved across the bridge of her nose. She didn't want to imagine what it might be. For the first time she was glad that her small light shed just enough illumination to guide her several feet at a time. She wasn't sure she wanted to see what was ahead. Her only solace was the cool breeze. Even though the air was musty and damp, it still contained plenty of oxygen for her hungry lungs.

Emma didn't know how long she had been in the cavern. She rubbed the sore spot on the back of her head. How long had she been knocked out? She patted the front of her shirt to make sure the folder of papers and ledger was still there, buttoned next to her skin.

She had to save the papers. No matter what.

Gradually, the dank air began to take on a different scent. Was she really starting to smell roses and pine trees or was she hallucinating? Maybe it was like a mirage in the desert. Maybe she was losing her mind. Maybe there wasn't enough oxygen after all. Her mind raced. "You have to calm down, Emma," she told herself firmly. Becoming hysterical now would just make matters worse. And she had to get out of here. There was much more at stake than her own life. She continued moving ahead and after a few more minutes her efforts were rewarded. She lifted the light above her head and gasped with relief and joy. This was not a hallucination! Her penlight reflected a wall—not of dirt and stone—but of thick green leaves and delicate red rose blossoms!

"Thank you, Lord!" she called out to the sky as she pushed her way through the branches and twigs into the open air. Her legs were shaky as she slowly coaxed them to stand upright. Where was she? The place looked familiar, but she was still dazed from her narrow escape and her long, cramped journey, and had trouble putting her surroundings into context. She could see a long line of pine trees and a stone wall with the climbing roses. Bertha's roses! Of course. She was at the back side of the Brubaker garden wall, just next to the mansion!

She looked around to the opening of the tunnel she had made when she pushed her way through. There was that symbol again, the compass rose, etched into the stone wall. She couldn't believe it. Who could have imagined that a tunnel was hidden beneath the bramble of roses?

The wind suddenly shifted direction, and the scent of roses was overpowered by the acrid smell of smoke. The library! thought Emma in a panic. It might be burning down! She forced her trembling legs to move forward in the direction of the Custer's Mill Library.

She was greeted by the sight of tanker trucks and heavily suited firemen. Frantically, she scanned the crowd for a familiar face. Was Jake there? Would he have been at Aunt Mia's already? She began to run toward the building but was stopped by a young man wearing a reflective vest. "Sorry, ma'am. You can't go any nearer."

"Emma!" Mia's voice was a mixture of disbelief and hysteria as she caught a glimpse of her niece. "Is that really you?"

Emma tried to smile but burst into tears instead. "Oh Aunt Mia, it was horrible! And now the library is burning! Where's Jake? I need to talk to Jake!" Emma was vaguely aware that her words were coming out in a jumble, but she was powerless to stop them.

"The last time I saw Jake he was talking with the fire chief." Mia led Emma toward a man in a smoky red suit. "Sir, this is my niece, Emma! She isn't in the building after all!" The man glanced at the two women and grabbed his pager. "Cancel the alert. Person in question is not in the building." He snapped the plastic communication device shut and glared at Mia. "Ma'am, you should get your facts straight before you go putting our men's lives in danger."

"What's going on here, Captain?" Emma recognized a familiar voice. Jake! Not thinking beyond the present moment, or even considering the muddy, disheveled state she was in, she ran straight into his arms. He stroked her head and murmured into her matted hair. "Oh, Emma! I was so afraid I had lost you, too!'

Emma's head rested against Jake's chest. She felt safe. But then the immediacy of the situation came back to her in a flash. She couldn't stay here. Not yet. "Jake! Where's Pete? He tried to kill me and I think he had something to do with Bertha's murder!" She began to pull papers from the folder still stuck inside her shirt.

Chapter 48

Pete skidded across the gravel as he slammed on the brakes. How in Hades had she escaped? His police radio confirmed that she had. That Kramer woman was invincible. Well, no time to think about it now. His life was on the skids. Worse than that. He was a ruined man—at least here in this one-horse town.

The best he could hope for was to get the heck out of Dodge. Get far enough away so he could start over again. He slammed the truck door and started toward his house. Suddenly, he heard a cough from the direction of the porch. He wasn't alone. He cursed under his breath. There was Shep sitting on his front step. Pete wasn't sure about much at the moment, but he was sure he was done with this sniveling idiot. Shep had been his puppet long enough. He could be thrown on the discard pile now. He glared at the other man as he walked toward him.

"Tough goin'," said Shep hesitantly.

Pete spat on the driveway. "What're you doing here, Shep? Go home. Your services are no longer needed."

"Whatdya mean?" Shep looked nervous.

"Just get outta here. That Kramer chick escaped the library somehow. It's over, Shep. I'm gone and you're on your own."

"But how did she, I mean, didn't you lock her in? That was the plan!"

"I don't know how she got out. I don't care how she got out. I need to save my own hide now and I don't have time for the likes of you!" Pete's stride lengthened as he neared the house.

"But we've always stuck together, boss! You can't leave me alone now!" Shep was almost pleading.

Pete turned around and walked to within inches of Shep's face. "Now listen here, buddy, I don't take kindly to associating myself with murderers. You're a killer, Shep! You killed old lady Brubaker by giving her that potion from your grandmother, and you tried to kill that nutcase Hiram. And then there's the kidnapping . . . You're gonna hang."

Shep leaned against the porch rail and struggled to speak. "But we're friends, Pete, right? I was just doing what you told me to do. The plan—you remember—the plan!"

"Get out of my way!" Pete pushed Shep away and slammed the door behind him. He emerged a few minutes later carrying a box and dragging a suitcase behind him. Shep had already disappeared.

Pete turned the key, his foot already on the gas pedal. Shifting into reverse, he gunned the four-wheel drive out of the driveway and then immediately slammed on the brakes. Revolving blue lights surrounded him, and the shrill sounds of sirens pierced the night air. Pete put his head on the steering wheel and let out a string of profanity just as Jake stepped out of the cruiser.

"Get out of the truck, Anderson."

Pete rolled down the window. "Now, Jake. This isn't what it looks like. You've got it all wrong! Shep Crawford's your man."

"Get out of the truck. Now." For the first time, Pete noticed that Jake held a revolver in his right hand. "Hands in the air; step out slowly. It's over, Anderson."

EPILOGUE

Wednesday, July 4, 2012

A gray early morning had given way to a crisp, blue sky. White cotton clouds bounced and collided with each other on the western horizon. The air had lost some of its early July humidity. It was turning out to be a perfect day for a Fourth of July celebration.

Nanette squirted a spiral of whipped cream over the tops of two lightly browned cherry pies and put them in her picnic basket. She wiped her hands on a kitchen towel and picked up the wicker container. Time to head over to the park for the festivities.

The gazebo in the center of the park was draped in patriotic streamers, and the picnic tables spread across the lawn alternated red, white, and blue covers. Hoyt and Reba were lugging a huge cooler filled with ice and Jane was lining up the food on serving tables.

"Here you go, Jane! Add these to your offerings." Nanette handed her the picnic basket and went over to inspect the rest of the food. "Looks like Custer's Mill folks outdid themselves this year. I won't need to eat for a week after today."

"I think we're all so grateful that Emma is safe and our library building is saved from that awful fire."

Nanette swatted at a swarm of gnats. "Don't get me wrong. I'm glad young Emma didn't get hurt by that good-for-nothing ex-police chief, but I think it's kinda ironic that our library was saved from the fire only to be torn down!"

"You don't know that," said Jane as she placed a large silver spoon in a bowl of yellow potato salad. "We haven't heard the final verdict yet."

"Final verdict on what, dear ladies?" Professor Nelson placed a pan of crispy rolls on the table and smiled.

"You didn't bake those, did you, Al?" Nanette looked at the elderly man with suspicion.

The professor smiled. "No, I'm afraid my culinary skills are limited to boiling water for tea and opening packs of crackers. I stopped by the bakery and picked these up on the way here. They smell heavenly."

"What verdict were you talking about?" asked the professor, not to be drawn off his original course. "Is someone on trial?"

"Not yet," said Nanette, looking across the park as people began to trickle in for the celebration. "I just told Jane that it's ironic that the library was saved from the fire only to be torn down by the highway engineers."

"I'm afraid the highway engineers will have to reroute their new road," said the professor quietly. "There is no judge in the land that will allow them to tear down a nationally registered historic building!" He held up a document and waved it triumphantly.

"Are you serious, Al? Did we get the documentation?"

"It's all right here in black and white! We used to have to fill out forms, send them via the US Postal Service and wait. Now, with online forms, we can get the transaction made within days instead of weeks."

To her embarrassment, Nanette felt her eyes well up. She grabbed the professor and gave him a long hug.

"Careful now, dear lady," gasped the professor. "I'm an old man. My ribs are brittle and my heart is weak!" But he had a broad smile on his face.

"So when are you going to make the announcement, Professor Nelson?" Jane took a swipe at her red-rimmed eyes and smiled.

"I thought maybe just before we offer thanks for the food. Hoyt has requested that I ask the blessing. Perhaps I will make the announcement just before so we can all have one more thing for which to be thankful."

"If we're counting things to be thankful for, I've got something to add." Sissy's face was flushed and she was slightly out of breath. But she was beaming as she struggled to push a wheelchair over a clump of grass. "I've got my daddy back! And," she added, "I'm thankful that the poison Shep or Pete poured down his throat didn't kill him."

"Say what?" asked Nanette. "Somebody tried to poison Hiram?"

"You don't have to talk like I wasn't here," came a querulous voice from the wheelchair. "Yeah. Somebody tried to poison me. Not just somebody. Those workers of iniquity; those evil men in high places. And now Shep's on the run. Probably hidin' out in a cave somewhere."

"Boy that Pete Anderson sure had me fooled! I thought he was a decent lawman." Lula moved closer to Hiram. "I never thought I'd say this, but I'm sure glad to see your grizzly old face. I should just plant a big, juicy kiss right on that stubbly cheek!"

Hiram jerked his head away. "Take me away from this place, girl. I am being pursued by a wanton woman." Although the tone of his voice hadn't changed, those standing close by could see a twinkle in his eye.

"So that's what it was. Poison." Professor Nelson stood with his hand on Hiram's shoulder. "Probably the same mixture they used on Bertha. "I wonder . . ." His voice trailed off.

"Well we're glad you're still with us," said Nanette. "We're going to be needing a gardener at our newly acquired piece of property. We don't know what the heck we're going to do with it yet, but we do know those rose gardens will remain in tip-top shape. As a memorial to Bertha. Least we could do."

Hiram nodded gravely. "We might work out a deal. I'm right grateful to be alive." He passed a weathered hand over his face. "Clever of that Anderson and Crawford to make it look like I'd taken to drinking. Clever, but not clever enough. Reckon we have a decent detective in town now. Guess I owe my life to Jake Preston."

"What's this? Y'all congregating without a permit?" Billy came to join the group. He clamped a hand on Hiram's arm. "Awful good to see you, man."

Hiram grunted.

"I know I've been a jerk for a lot of years, Hiram. Guess it started way back in high school. You know I owe you big time. I should have spoken up for you thirty years ago after that Fourth of July mess."

Hiram turned his face away from Billy and squinted into the sun. "Yeah, maybe you should've."

"You spent time in jail for something you didn't do."

"You think I don't know that, Mr. High and Mighty Town Manager?" Hiram's voice was angry. "You think I don't know what really happened?"

Billy's face was a conflict of emotions. "You know I was crazy about her. Kath, I mean. And her momma wouldn't let me hang around—probably because she didn't like that rascal, Pete, who was pretending to be my friend at the time. Anyway, it was Pete's idea to scare Ruth by burning down that little shed. We didn't mean to catch the house on fire. And we certainly didn't know Kath was in there." Billy's voice broke.

Professor Nelson took a silk handkerchief from his pocket and wiped his eyes.

Hiram turned to face Billy. "Be sure your sins will find you out."

Billy sighed. "My sins not only found me out, they've haunted me for almost thirty years. Haunted me in the form of Pete Anderson. He had me convinced that I was the one who killed Kath. That it was my firecracker that set the house on fire. Maybe it was, maybe it wasn't. I guess we'll never know.

"What I do know is that I'm done with lies. Done with hiding and done with guilt. I paid Pete Anderson a hefty sum of money every month for almost three decades. Got him the police chief job. Paid him to keep his mouth shut. But it's over now. And it's high time to move on." Billy walked closer to the wheelchair and knelt down beside Hiram. "I know this is a lot to ask. I know I don't deserve it, but can you find it in your heart to forgive me, Hiram?"

The air was silent except for the buzzing of a honeybee. It seemed as though all of nature was silent, waiting for the verdict. Waiting for Hiram's answer.

Finally, he spoke, softly at first, but with gathering strength. "I'm not gonna lie, Brubaker. I don't like you very much. I probably never will. But I will tell you this. I don't go with holding a grudge either. Miss Bertha trusted me. She hired lawyers to get me out of jail. For her sake, I'll make a truce with you."

Billy grinned. "I won't ask you to shake my hand right now. Maybe we can work up to that."

"Don't expect miracles, Brubaker. I'm still a weak man." Hiram's face relaxed into a trace of a smile.

The night sky erupted in bursts of gold, green, and violet as the fireworks sizzled through the air. Jake and Emma sat on a picnic blanket and watched the display of Custer's Mill's finest pyrotechnics. The explosions echoed across the nearby mountains.

"Do they always have such an impressive show?" Jake leaned back on one elbow and looked up at Emma.

"They're usually pretty good, but I think this year has topped them all."

"We have a lot to celebrate this summer," said Jake, quietly.

"It has been quite a month," agreed Emma. She closed her eyes and tried to shut out the sight of Pete's face leering down at her.

"Are you okay, Emma?" Jake sat up and took Emma's hand. "You still have some nasty scratches on your arm." He ran a light finger over a bandage.

"I'll be okay, Jake. I just need some time to process it all. Everything happened so fast."   "Indeed," said Jake. "So very fast."

"Hey Daddy!" The excited voice broke the spell. "Guess what?" Kate jumped down beside Jake and put her hands on both of his shoulders.

"What, punkin?" Jake let go of Emma's hand and held his daughter.

"Serafina's gonna teach me how to make a garland out of herbs and flowers! Right, Serafina?" Kate jumped up and tugged on Serafina's long, flowing skirt.

"Watch out, gal, this skirt is just held up by elastic!" She gave Jake an amused smile.

Emma was annoyed at this interruption. She attempted a smile. "That will be so much fun, Kate! You can be a real princess!"

Another burst of fireworks lit the sky, and then all was silent. After a few moments, the voice of Town Manager Billy Brubaker came over the loudspeaker. "Ladies and gentlemen, our grand finale will begin in a moment, but before we set off our last and brightest fireworks, I— um—want to take a minute to thank each of you for coming this evening."

There was a long pause, and Billy seemed to be trying to decide what to say. "I know a lot of bad stuff has happened in our town in the past couple of weeks. I know part of it has been my fault. Right now, I would like to—um—like to tell you how sorry I am for everything. I never meant for this whole road project to go this far. I always hoped something would happen to stop it. Most of what happened was out of my control, but I thank those of you who were able to bring our town back to the way it should be. I know I've probably made a mess out of more than just my speech this evening. But I'm sorry. And I thank you for your kindness and forgiveness."

Billy stepped down from the podium just as the final booms reverberated, and a burst of light shot up into the heavens.

"Wow!" whispered Kate. "It's magic!"

Emma felt a sense of peace there on this hillside surrounded by the dark silhouettes of the members of her community. Most folks were staring at the sky, eyes planted on the display of color that was piercing the dark clouds.

And then the air changed ever so slightly. The breeze shifted to the east causing the poplar leaves to crackle like the rustling of fine silk. A slight movement caught Emma's eye, and for a split second, she thought she could see the small, stooped form of a woman standing off to the side.

And for just one moment, she was quite certain she caught a whiff of peach roses.

About the Author

Mary Fulk Larson is

- Mary M. Smith, Ed.D., who enjoyed a thirty-year career as a public school teacher, university professor, and curriculum developer, and now offers her services to community and church organizations;
- Tammy Fulk Cullers, M.A. Ed., who teaches middle school English, grows low-maintenance plants, plays piano and collects green glass; and
- Barbara Larson Finnegan, M.B.A., a master gardener and CFO of a small publishing company where she wears a variety of hats.

Cumulatively, the authors have ten grown children and ten grandchildren, and live with their husbands in the lovely Shenandoah Valley.

L to R: Barbara Finnegan, Mary Smith, Tammy Cullers